THE BLINK THAT KILLED THE EYE

THE BLINK THAT KILLED THE EYE

Anthony Anaxagorou is an acclaimed poet, prose writer, playwright, performer and educator. He has published eight volumes of poetry, a spoken word EP and written for theatre. His poetry has appeared on BBC Youth Nation, BBC Newsnight, the British Urban Film Awards, BBC 6 Music and been performed by Cirque du Soleil. He teaches poetry and creative writing in schools, and works closely with both The Poetry Society and First Story. His work has been studied in universities across the USA, UK and Australia, as well as being translated into Spanish, Japanese and French.

www.anthonyanaxagorou.com

Also by Anthony Anaxagorou

Poetry

Card Not Accepted
Poems to Maya
Pale Remembered
The Lost Definition of Hope
Let This Be The Call
Returning Stranger
Sad Dance
A Difficult Place to Be Human

EP

It Will Come To You

THE BLINK THAT KILLED THE EYE

and other stories

Anthony Anaxagorou

JACARANDA
LONDON

First published in Great Britain in 2014 by
Jacaranda Books Art Music Ltd
5 Achilles Road
London NW6 1DZ
www.jacarandabooksartmusic.co.uk
Copyright © Anthony Anaxagorou, 2014

1

Typeset by James Nunn.
Printed and bound in Great Britain by CPI.

A CIP catalogue record for this book is available from the British Library.

ISBN: 9781909762046
eISBN: 9781909762107

The paper this book is printed on is certified by the (c) 1996 Forest
Stewardship Council A.C. (FSC). It is ancient-forest friendly. The printer
holds FSC chain of custody SGS-COC-2061.

For Sabrina Mahfouz

In a very ordinary world
A most extraordinary pain mingles with the small routines,
The loss seems huge and yet
Nothing can be pinned down or fully explained.

Brian Patten

Contents

Bad Company   15

Keep Still   31

Building Six   41

Have You Ever Seen A Big Man Fall?   67

Yellow Daffodil   73

Cowboy   93

Belongings   109

The Blink That Killed The Eye   123

Last Lament   163

Acknowledgements   169

Bad Company

It's always during moments like this, amidst the slapping wind, bitter frustration and utter powerlessness that I think back to my father. Know your worth is what he would say. A conservative tie primly crossed at the point where his throat would tighten to speak, only ever allowing itself to loosen after an essential stream of whiskey had taken to relax his blood. He lived alone, my parents deciding to divorce the year before I started secondary school. Sallow lighting hung around the unkept corners of the modest room he rented. He had no friends and cared little for sports or anything involving teams. He would constantly stress that people spoke too much. Fervently he would say how everyone held opinions and agendas that only served to compensate for what their lives were really lacking.

Stay focused.

He kept no pets and watered no plants, admitting both required a love he was unable to provide. When it came to music and literature however he was more than capable of generating an exclusive, spacious heart where both could be accommodated. I would always leave him feeling more and more confused. On the one hand he loathed opinion and similarly the opinionated, yet on the other that's all he was, a non-active, contradictory set of theories and beliefs. His bare and laconic style of interaction would cause whatever he expressed to linger for unhealthy periods of time on the bleak shores of my young consciousness. In our life we all die many times Alex, it's the last death we need to be most worried about. What did that even mean?

Often when he would begin speaking on subjects of life and purpose I would be hunched in one of the corners of his room, ranting in cynical bursts about whatever menial or demoralising job I happened to be under at the time. He would sit pensively, listening, but never with his eyes. His gaze would slowly coast away to meet some invisible creature out beyond his single window, or he would stare vacuously into the palms of his hands, never looking at me. Then astonishingly, once I'd finished his response would somehow be the most concise, the most elucidating and insightful solution or token of advice anyone could have offered me. Poised and aloof he may have appeared, especially to those who first encountered him, but contrary to the assumption they may have formed he was in fact one of the most perceptive and astute characters I had ever known. He simply had a way of doing things in strict accordance with his own set of principles, and society will forever detest and chastise people like that.

It wasn't until I was older that I was fully able to comprehend what it meant to be present while simultaneously appearing absent in a world crowded with noise and commotion. That's how his memory works on me now, coming back to present itself whenever I'm left waiting like this, my uncle having gone off to run yet another errand. Once the monotony starts to take effect I find myself rummaging through the moments we had together, unearthing a little relief from those aphoristic penchants he would so readily share. Most recently I've been thinking back to the evening we spoke about worth. Him sitting with a single-malt whiskey in his hand, the few remaining tassels of white hair sparsely covering his head. The crows-feet imprinted on his deep eyes spreading and pushing down into his skin at the moment something made him smile, proof that even happiness wants to be acknowledged in the sad history of the face. A quaint lamp bending its light to fit into each uneven crevice making it all seem like sets of individual pages from a great book, one reaching its end but that you desperately need to go on forever. His arms resting over the chair, erudite and boss-like. Know your worth Alex, that's all you'll ever need to recognise. Everything else can be learnt from books or life, but worth, that's something only you can decide.

The winds are picking up. The sky's overcast. The trees look like old derelict buildings. I'm holding it down. The fourth edge of the blue tarpaulin we put up to act as a low makeshift roof while we build the wall for the top part of his house. My uncle's house. It'll become part of an extension he's planning on converting into a small office, at least that's what he tells me. I'm pressing down into the corner. Firmly. It's not even high enough to stand up in but I don't ask questions. We're out of nails again, he's only got screws, which he says can't be used to fasten the plastic sheet into the wood so he needs to go and buy another packet. It feels like being inside a cheap tent we've pitched up at the summit of some undiscovered mountain. The corner I'm crouched in is littered with solidified remnants of cement and scattered wood shavings. A mess. My knees are becoming sore and bruised again. He's had to go to the B&Q down the road. Again. The only instruction he left me with was to hold my corner down until he came back. Again. To not let go or it'll take us another hour to try and put the tarpaulin back up. To not fuck up Alex. Again. This is all time we don't have. Remember what happened the other day? I'm looking around nervously at the unmanned edges. A pile of stacked bricks on one. Another load stacked on the adjacent corner. Those were all the spare bricks we had up here so we improvised using a drill and a chunky hammer defaced with white paint-speckles to act as the weight for the third corner. I've been holding it down, the fourth corner, my corner, for over five minutes now. He knows I could mess it up like I've done before, he knows I'm an amateur hence why he scampered down the ladder like running water shouting I'll be back in fifteen minutes. Don't let me down Al!

The two wooden beams we put up in the middle of the roof to keep the tarpaulin erect are teetering with each new gust of wind. If I do let go and he comes back to find the same mishap as last week then he'll fire me on the spot. We had the same issue then; only my back gave in minutes after he'd left. My arms started to shake, my leg muscles trembled and before I knew it my body was trying to pull itself apart as the roof collapsed around me. Pathetic really because it took us forty-five minutes to put the whole thing back up again, then another forty-five minutes to take it down at the end of the day. He scorned bitterly that the time altogether cost him £200, threatening to deduct it from my wages although he never did. Instead he proceeded to moan and cuss for thirty of those forty-five minutes, blasting the overall circumstance of things; his fate, his luck, rich people, corrupt politicians and then his ex-wife, concluding at last with the omnipotent God he ardently prayed to each night. For the remaining fifteen minutes he swore directly at me, cursing my idleness and incompetence. Combined within those insults was his view on my general lack of ability to do anything to an even slightly satisfactory standard. If I were to lie I would say his chiding assessment didn't really bother me, but I won't lie. In fact, now that I can feel myself becoming increasingly anxious at the possibility of the same situation repeating, I'm forced to recall another recent error, one that caused him again to lose his temper with me.

The day before last I made a cement mix but it was too loose. Again, it was my fault. I ended up adding too much water into the mix by mistake. I wasn't paying attention. He couldn't use a mix like that for the wall. In a mad annoyance he dashed the bucket off the roof, slashes of grey runny soup painting the dead grass below. My mind was elsewhere. I tried to explain that to him in the most honest way possible, but he screamed out saying he didn't give a shit, and I should come to work with a clear, focused head. He said he wasn't paying me to constantly blunder his work, which as he always reminded me would cost him both time and money. He's right, it's his business and his house we're fixing up after all but here's the truth of it, I mainly think about her. I think of where we've come from and where we might be heading but without the common fondness you might expect to find attached to such a personal and honest confession.

Change hands.

Stretch out the fingers.

Keep strong.

Watch your back.

I'm thinking now if I accidentally do let go again and he comes back to shout, or even call me what he did a few days ago, I'll probably leave. Leaving any kind of relationship takes a substantial amount of courage, a sure mustering of strength and self-worth both of which I've always seemed to lack. I don't think there's been a time when I haven't backed away from some sort of physical confrontation or challenge. As a young boy I would be content to stand inert and unguarded while the onslaught of punches from whoever had taken issue with me would proceed to cut my skin, burst open my lip and blacken my eyes. Back then it seemed far easier to stand and do nothing than to go through the daring ordeal of retaliating with my own series of feeble strikes. Plus, I never regarded myself as a fighter, what with my spindly legs and uncoordinated arms. From then I accepted I would make a skill out of endurance rather than aggression. In class, teachers would scorn me and again I'd do little to stand up for myself. Instead I'd sit surreptitiously at my desk, my face appearing more amazed at their fervent contempt for one so young and blameless than for the brazen reproach of my averse way. Back at home cousins would ridicule everything I came to like about myself which soon enough worked its way into successfully undoing any bit of self-admiration I may have been fortunate enough to establish.

That's when my back gave way. I was having these very thoughts when I felt a sharp spasm-like twinge attack me, followed by the ataxic withdrawal of motion and stability; finally to be crushed by the collapse, feeling the cold wet ground against my clothes. I couldn't move. Agony. There was nobody to call. If you've been unfortunate enough to experience muscle spasms or have trapped nerves toss your limbs into rolls of stiff relentless whirls, then you'll know it's not the burning sensation in the shoulders or the sequential throbbing that drives the overall discomfort. It's the rigorous trapping in the lower part of the body, the ongoing relentless pangs leaving you groaning in excruciating pain shamed on the floor, prostrate and weird like some marooned starfish. That's how I must have looked to him when he came back up the ladder with the packet of nails in his hand, to find me wriggling and my body gripped with pain. I'd raised the issue with him before.

The other afternoon he had me carry two buckets of brick-mix up to the roof at the same time. A bucket in each hand whilst trying to climb a ladder. Imagine. For two hours straight. Each one must have weighed around 12kg. After the second hour I admitted, defeated, I couldn't do it anymore. My hands were raw and calloused and my back was aching to the point it hurt to stand straight. He retorted mockingly saying it was due to the amount of time I'd spent reading books. According to him it had nothing to do with the weight of the brick-mix or the taxing duration of the labouring. Too much looking down he sneered. Too much looking down and sitting in front of those devil screens. He may have had a point. Whenever I happened to be on lunch or waiting for new instructions I'd pull out whatever book I was reading, this was my preferred way of filling the unpredictable gaps between hours. It was either that or stand idly kicking gravel until he decided what it was he wanted me to do. My jobs weren't particularly exciting either. They mainly ranged from mixing cement, carrying bricks from one place to another, emptying sacks of debris into the skip, cleaning out the back of his van or running to the shops if he needed another packet of cigarettes. I've always enjoyed reading.

Poetry, I was to soon discover, had a special reverence within such a disorderly working environment. Its economy meant I was able to dip in and out of pieces without having to follow the particularly long and complex narratives common to most novels. Sometimes I would read the same poem for days, continually discovering something new and appealing. Then, if I wanted to change things up I'd bring in stories, even essays or other non-fictional writing along with a flask of green tea and some sandwiches. Very quickly they too became like spectacular films I could watch on my imagination's screen. He'd tell me reading was for people who didn't know how to live, that's why they were so engrossed in the lives of all those characters that didn't really exist.

There will come a point in your life where you'll be forced to make some decisions Alex. To travel into those parts of yourself you fear most. That's what true bravery is. To go where the lights are broken and the only voice you can make out is your own ugly rebound. Those will be the moments which go on to shape your life. I'm ten minutes in. I'm doing alright so far. I'm being cautious. You see Alex, decisions involving bravery can catapult you out of one reality and straight into another if you let them, sometimes for the worse but sometimes for the better. I'm doing good. I'm feeling strong. Only another five minutes and he'll be back.

One evening I came home from school with a split lip and a cut eye. My father asked me what happened. I must have been about eight when I told him for the first time that I wasn't brave. That I didn't like fighting and all the other boys were stronger and more aggressive than me. I told him I liked reading and how the friends I made in books were far nicer than the ones I made in school. He stubbed out his cigarette tilting my head up towards the celling, moving my eye into the light so as to see the depth of the cut. Your mother will be upset. How many? Just one I replied staring up at him, a tremble in my throat. So why didn't you hit the bastard back? Because he was bigger than me and I was scared. He took a breath in turning away to wade off his frustration. Your granddad used to tell me that we were peaceful people living in a violent place. I was the same at your age but there's only so much the eyes can take before all they're able to see is dirt. He walked out the room, leaving me to wash the dried blood off my face with a hot towel by the sink. For most young boys that would have been the moment when the next encounter with a bully would result in some kind of assailed retaliation. Not for me though. I wasn't that strong. I never could hit back.

It's pouring down with all the confidence of heaven now. One of the beams has fallen. The other three corners seem to be slowly losing their fight too. He's been gone for nearly twenty minutes. He's doing it to me again. My fingers are starting to ache turning a light blue against their bones. Take one hand off. Put the other hand on. Flex. Rotate. Keep it together. Put pressure where it's needed. In the corner. Strength. Stamina. Strength. Stamina.

Since working here I've found myself writing more. My friend Wilton who's a literature aficionado mentioned there were nights in town where people could go to read their work. After some deliberation I decided to take myself along and find the confidence to recite a few pieces I'd recently put together. The people there didn't speak much to each other which suited me fine. In a safe corner I sat discretely knowing nobody would come to bother me. I signed up for the open-mic. The host, a tall angular man with brown eccentric hair and a waistcoat matching his shoes giving him the appearance of being fashionably odd, told the tense anxious crowd it didn't matter if others understood the poems or not, the point of the night was for people to come and read free of judgment and criticism. He also stipulated humorously that poems couldn't be maliciously directed at other poets in the audience, saying it had happened before in the past. The crowd found this amusing, a low rumble of shy laughter gently swallowing each person's nerves, whereas I stayed too contorted to pay it any real attention.

Wilton mentioned how many great writers began reading their work at nights such as these. Poets, novelists, playwrights, all reciting sections of their stories and poems to random audiences. He told me how at the end of each reading the crowd would applaud out of sheer politeness, so if I was to read I shouldn't see the gesture as the barometer with which to gauge the success of my writing. The piece I thought to perform was one I'd written linking the process of building a wall to the art of crafting a poem.

From the outset walls can appear quite disenchanting and average, similar to the way a poem can, but with closer inspection they both have the ability to transcend the ordinary. It was only after labouring for these months that I began to see how a wall is in actual fact the ancient poetry of stone. Architects, builders and bricklayers are in a sense all creating an alternative kind of poetry. Each brick acts like a single word, one constantly relying on the other to properly define it, then line by line, its shape and form is provided by the structure it finally comes to stand inside. From what I've understood poetry is more about the words a writer doesn't use than those she or he does use, just like the bricklayers who at their disposal have a limited number of bricks which they use to build the wall that eventually becomes the impenetrable body of the entire building. They will cut away at parts too wide in the same way a poet will refrain from using words which are unable to fit around the abstract images of the mind – manipulating tenses and grammatical categories which in turn will give birth to new definitions and concepts, those which were previously unheard of. Hunched over their wall the inward bricklayers depend on the learned arithmetic and symmetry of their straining eyes, while across the road the working poet may too be sat hunched at his or her keyboard, pulling at those inventive aesthetics, playing with the various forms of metre so intrinsic in giving the writing its distinct pattern and velocity.

I read the piece to Wilton; he liked it. I think the audience did too despite them applauding me in the same sluggish manner they did the elderly gentleman who gave the impassioned outpouring of several short poems themed solely around bugs. Overall the night was a success, I jumped on the last train home in high spirits and for the first time in months I wasn't thinking about her or the building site.

Twenty-five minutes have gone. The remaining wooden beam is swaying stubbornly around the wind and rain. I look down into the garden. The ladder. No sign of him. The lower part of my back's beginning to release a slight tingle. Focus on something else. Something without pain. At around fifteen minutes after midnight I arrived home. She was already in bed. She liked to sleep but she didn't like to sleep alone. I put the television on mute, moving some of her paintings off the coffee table to place them carefully against the wall. They were still drying. Flicking to the wildlife channel I made myself a cup of chamomile tea in the usual ritualistic way. For the first time in as long as I can remember my whole body felt as if it were smiling. My mind still in that little poetry basement, filled with cheerful people who only wished to say nice things to one another. How amazing it would be to wake up each day and write. Then I started thinking of work and of labouring again; soon my meagre fantasy retreated back into my mind's private box. The rain's coming in directly now. Hitting my face. The first edge has twisted itself loose – the one with the drill and rusty hammer over it. There's nothing I can do. I look around at the other two corners and notice the intermittent gusts trying to tackle the helpless stack of bricks. I panic a useless panic. Know your worth he said. What am I even doing here? She wakes from her sleep shuffling into the living room to ask where I was. I tell her about the poetry show. The old man with his poems about bugs. How Wilton had suggested I should go to read. How they gave me an applause. She presses two fingers into each of her temples. Massaging. Closing both eyes. Keeping the pressure on. She asks when I'm coming to bed. I say after the documentary. I ask her to sit down and watch it with me. I tell her it's about endangered species knowing how much she loves animals. She doesn't respond, keeping the pressure on her temples. I ask if she wants a herbal tea. She takes the two fingers off her head to rest them on her hips. Her thick white dressing gown half undone exposing her blue nighty with a colourful Disney character I'm unfamiliar with. She's not wearing slippers. She tells me to come to bed. I explain how I'm just trying to let the adrenaline from the show settle then I'll come. The countenance on her face caves inwards. She says I'm neglecting her again. Not showing her enough love. That my poetry and my books are what's really important to me. I assure her that's not the case. Her voice grows louder. Fierce. She's no longer dazed and soft from sleep. My voice falls lower. Whispering. I mention the neighbours. We shouldn't shout. I remind her of the couple downstairs with the baby. She ignores me. Her eyes becoming wet and dangerous. On the other side of the roof the first stack of bricks comes undone. Two wild edges of tarpaulin are now whipping themselves against the fury of the storm. I look at the solitary beam of wood trying to support the precarious structure. It's still there although now it looks weak and afraid. The rain pelts relentlessly. I'm drenched. Cold. The sky is a warship grey. I shiver. Storming towards the coffee table she picks up my mug of chamomile tea, the television flashing muted images of a group of fishermen off the Japanese coast spearing a family of terrified whales. The last remaining corner has three bricks on it. It's looking strong. Hope redefines itself. I'm contemplating using my foot to pin down my corner so as I can try and put the drill, hammer and fallen bricks back on top of their sides. I don't know if I can stretch myself all the way across. I put my foot down. She picks up the mug of boiling tea and throws it in my face. I shoot up from the sofa. Panicked. Screaming. In pain. She smashes the mug over the side of my head, just above my right ear. Her paintings fall flat on the floor as if too beautiful to witness such ugliness. I grab her wrist. I'm unable to reach over to the bricks. They're too far away. The roof is too wide. Too big. Bigger than me. I can see the blue plastic slipping away. I lunge back to my corner and push down hard with both hands. Everything hurts. I feel sick. Tears discover my eyes. I throw her onto the floor howling down into her face. My head pressed down hard onto hers. Hot saliva splattering after each syllable. Blood ruins what's left of her infuriated beauty. She screams her nose is broken again. She kicks me in the stomach. I fall back into the wall. Looking at her. At the blood. I say I'm sorry. I'm so so sorry. That I didn't do it deliberately. I hold back tears but my eyes crack. I try to explain how she pushed me. I reacted badly. That she smashed a mug over my head first and I would never have hurt her intentionally. She runs over to the bathroom to look in the mirror. I push down harder. Cursing. Hot saliva splattering after each syllable. I can't tell the difference between tears and rain. My body shudders. Her nose is fine. She feels it all over. Looking for blood or bone. Nothing's broken. She stands in front of the mirror baffled. Her face changes. Her mouth sinking as she says the words oh no and sorry repeatedly. Reaching out in a half-dead motion she touches the side of my head, the side gushing blood, then with both her hands cupped over her mouth she hastens out the front door, out into the blindness of the night. I replace her face in the mirror. I scream. I cry. For help. For assistance. I'm on my own. The only person here. The storm's all around and there's nobody with me.

I'm letting it all go. I can't.

I release.

The last beam drops like a shot-down guard as the blue tarpaulin soars up towards the sky with all the aggression of a wild thing, drifting back down to fall into the garden below where it wraps itself around the solid body of an old tree. I'm laying flat with my back against the cold roof looking up. The wooden beam dead and wet beside me. I see the rain as it should be seen, falling purposefully on my face – naked, cruel and dumb. Stretching out my lower back I attempt to expel the pain, steadily trying to breathe, closing both my eyes waiting for my uncle to return.

Keep Still

Father, since your death I have come to know the weight of his metal, and all its hopeless magic. The way it loathes gravity. How it exasperates the stitches of respect that could exist between two people. Each night the darkness unpacks itself keeping the distressed shape of all my secrets. How it can grip them by the throat, whispering death in the language of sweat-filled fists, of intoxicated madness spurred on by shadows that bark, while a curled, meek woman prays to the God of air for salvation, for rescue. Most nights repeat. Repetition becomes life's supreme torturer. I believed you when you said this would be best for me. That I must go forward. That I would be safe with him, that our home would be a place I could leave all age in; raise children in, conflate dreams with adoration. In my mind it worked, like most things do before they get handed over to reality.

For so long I buried my anguish beneath the colour of each bruise he marked me with. Never could I find the courage to tell you. How would you respond? You were ill. Everyone knew. Your frailty. There's a war which rages on unreported. A war that will be given to no epoch, no book, no scholar's acumen. A war that murders the self. The invisible war inside the heart – this I know now. Everything learns the nature of dying, as we all must, but these sensations weren't to come until later, when he came, with all his thunderous ways, leaving them to blaze in the passivity of mine.

It's June and it's raining. Androgynous beads, malleable and blind, fall from cosmic darkness – the infinite roof of the world. The petrichor perfuming the wet skin of earth. At night I listen to the dissonant tune of his sleep. He's here and you're not. I find him sprawled out in the bed, alive, full-faced, round and distant, like some ancient monster mythology was too afraid to authenticate. Cryogenic blood, a beast that somehow came to elude extinction. It's strange, I remember you telling me when I was a girl that sleep was supposed to be peaceful. You said it worked as an impartial realm where the spirit could go to recalibrate and atone for the sins it might accumulate throughout the day. I see how his sleep appears to work as a hurricane incessantly reproducing itself. Over and over. Those deep heavy rocks lodged tight in his chest, screaming to get out. That bruised sky cracking in his throat. His body wet from the night's heat. Punishment. That's why I adore this breed of darkness. Not just for the uncomfortable way it disturbs his rest, but also for the unending times I've managed to scurry into its vast cloak, forcing my body into a trained stillness.

Afraid. I'm always afraid. When he's close, approaching home loaded with all the fine principles of hell. Scuttling,

I forge an alliance with the unseen corners of the flat, despite the hammer in his mammoth voice, despite the war-drum in his step I wait hidden. Away. Crouched. Still as a nun's prayer, for the moment he gives up the search, drifting away unsatisfied. At the turn of his sleep's sound I emerge from those unnamed shadows and weep back into the musky blanket I took refuge in. Not because of him or what he'll do to me tomorrow or what he did to me yesterday, but for the shame, the letdown, the gradual collapse of the dreams you made for me. I will come here to this very spot, where I'll think of you in this broken bracket of a home and I'll ruminate into the frozen pipes of my voice, until finally I lose hold of my eyes and wait for sleep to offer its ancient salvation – like a commander thrusting me into the rapture of all the unconsciousness of antiquity.

'Get up off the floor. Stop crying. Stop crying I said. You're gonna wake the fucking baby.'

But there is a hope. Your name father, your earth-filled name assures me that tomorrow will be warm and effulgently alive. Even if the summer rains want to hound, I'll be fine in the knowledge that beyond the turmoil your name exists high up where a single sun hangs like a religion seeking veneration, beautiful and golden in its hoisted luminescence. A sun that prohibits the dead from having to witness the malice of the world. To die is not to be at peace but to embody a formless spirit branded with two sleeping eyes which perfectly mitigate the eternal act of dying. He will go to work, to his flowers and gardens. Using the same brutish hands he handles me with, he will kneel to plant a thousand unborn things. There he will labour with friends and come lunchtime he will listen to the stories they tell of their wives. How living with them is a battle only warriors prevail in. He will eat. Crunch down on ripe fruits. Feel the weather in his thick hair. Wet his mouth on juice. He will speak of his great ambitions; how he could have amounted to more had circumstances favoured him. How he was destined for fortune had it not been for the draft hounding his neck. Then he will put my name, the one I share with my mother, under an unsweetened tooth, biting down to repeat, again and again, repetition is life's supreme torturer.

A few miles away from his hard exhalation I will be living with my own mute flowers, at home with a son, your grandson, in a garden he has no business in, a land where he holds no command. Leaning into the ears of the verdant vines, the ephemeral irises and tulips I'll whisper my stories and woes. I'll create cities where each life has a proper name, where animals are free to sing and flowers become the artists that paint the walls of the world. For that brief moment, contained within the basket of hour and dream, I will feel the earthy hand of something that loves me. I will join its journey to feel it traverse through the torn fibres of my reticence, until on a day unknown it will finally give itself to the shores of my white voice and I will bloom with every colour yet to be sighted and named. I may cry. Most days I do. But the tears of the day are not the same as those of the night. They are so much more brilliant. Cool and sure. Owned entirely by my own face. Cascading to water the dry soil where so much of this comfort is found, tucking it safely away, because tonight, on his return, a storm will dock and I will attempt to evade the dying again, the fatal lance of the invisibility only I know. You see father, my stars have all been marked and exiled. My moon hangs like a pierced mural leaking sulphuric blood into each of my new mornings. My voice, a dry whisper borrowing what it can from the ripped pockets of some cancerous lump. I am here but in thirds. I am night for us both, always.

He hasn't been home for two days. Sometimes he does this, stays away, saying the thought of coming home to me is nauseating. Depressing. The baby lives oblivious as babies are born blessed to be. He can never fully acknowledge the son he conscripted into this. The baby's facile smile, tender and easy in the way that yours used to be, but one conceived under the silent ducts of catatonic beatings and gnawings, of pulling and ramming within a theatre of appalling rain.

The flat is as clean as it always is. I walk over to the spare room, the one that stays forever empty but with sheets I still wash at the end of each week despite nobody having slept in them. I imagine the voices of people we both love, of family and friends reverberating like music off the walls. I imagine how the bed-sheets would look in the morning after people had slept in them, made love in them, dreamt in them. It's just gone seven and I must feed your grandson again. The one who on the day of his birth had you announce proudly that he looked so much like him but cried like me.

Outside, the night is the poor owner of a few struggling stars. I'm over at my window with baby Robert on my lap. He smiles when I feed him – toothless but with a full mouth. A happy mouth. People are beginning to arrive home from work. To the right I can see the Anderson family. She's standing by the stove cooking, dressed in a grey tracksuit – the kind someone might put on after having spent an hour exercising. He stands by the sink in a white shirt, Mr. Anderson, his collar loose and easy. His posture reminding me of yours during the days you would come home tired but satisfied, when I was just starting to grow aware of the subtle harmony two fine people can create between them. He washes something. I can't quite make it out, my view hindered by the angle they move into. Something gets said. His shoulders roll back in a fit of laughter. The tap streams. Whatever it is she's saying to him it seems light and jovial. Playfully he flicks the water from the end of a celery stick causing her face to scrunch in on itself, eliciting a lover's jaunty giggle. Daintily she swats his arm. Love always looks like a lie when it's not your own.

In the living room a young boy rocks back and forth, chuckling intermittently to the flicker of a cartoon on a television screen. I kiss Robert's warm forehead. I smile at something I don't want to understand. In about an hour the Anderson family will shut the curtains to their life and I will take the baby to bed, handing him over to those saccharine dreams. He is only months old and I'm yet to hear him cry during sleep. I will kneel over his cot, as if paying homage to the part of myself that's still unblemished and pure, the part still able to hold another's hand without the semblance of sewage and dirt. Where memory falls absent to the tattooed world of knuckles and flames.

'You and your fucking window! Keep still! Shut up or you'll wake the baby. Stop moving around. Look straight. Keep looking straight ahead you filthy fucking bitch! Good. Keep still I said or I'll bury you out in the garden, I swear to God!'

I can't hate you for leaving me here, how were you to know? I can't even hate him for what he makes of my body and blood. It wasn't your fault. The other night he caught me at the window. I knew he would. I couldn't find a place to hide in time. Cocaine makes him more vigilant than usual. The baby was asleep. I was in a daze looking out the window, at the neighbours cooking and talking. My fault. If I were to speak of his methods, the cruelty and function of his sickness I'm sure it would rob the peace from your grave, crumble the sky from under whatever heaven you sleep in. On that night, your grandson cried for the both of us, for the first time, toothless and purple-faced. Into each other we screamed while he ripped me apart with only the boiling rain watching on, sounding like a swarm of insects offering their useless musical to the blind stage of my window. You aren't to blame.

Soon, I will return to my job. To the offices. The corporate escalators of the ambition and endeavour you set for me.

My smile will be new. My clothes pressed and clean. This being the only part of your dream that is still speakable. The part that has yet to wear a nightmare. All will appear fine. My colleagues will speak of their beloved families, the achievements of their children and the successes of their husbands, partners and lovers. I will remain quiet up until they ask me about him, then the words I speak will resemble those that weave fairytales, those I read your grandson before bed. They will want to know about holidays and intimacies and I will give them a truth I've never known. They will ask why my hands tremble at the sound of rain and I will blame the wretchedness of the season.

The downpour has stopped. The warm street outside cleansed of its filth. I've put your grandson to bed and the Anderson's have closed the curtains to their home.

I put the radio on low.

The poetry in the song. The hymn inside the ballad. The distant choir of a love unfound.

I'll let you into a little secret shall I? Shall I Rupal? If you died tomorrow nobody would miss you. Nobody would give a shit. I'll be the only person at your funeral. Just me and the boy, nobody else.

I turn up the radio, opening the window fully.

You stupid cunt. Look at me. Look at me. Nobody wants you. Nobody will ever want you.

The music crescendos. Second chorus. I stand up on the table, the one where I write to you. Breathe in the full body of night. Climbing.

'You wanna do something do you? You want something to do? Throw yourself out of that fucking window. Go on, see if you can fly. I dare you. Do it. Learn to fly, for me.'

One foot scuffs the other. Edging sideways. Both palms flatly pressed against the wall. Barefoot. Leave slippers on the bedroom floor. Night in between my toes. In my hair. Bones. On the ledge looking down. Shaking. Unsteady.

'Keep still!'

Keep still.

The baby cries something new. Like a siren. A wail. A dangerous call aimed only at me. Made from the ambulance of the lungs I gave him. Lungs that at one point would expand and fill then push and kick in fear while my baby remained trapped inside me, wanting escape, wanting end. For one so young he's been here before. He knows this place. Stop. Please stop. No more. Please. No more. His mother's lungs. Then, in the space of seconds, I see myself. My name. Your name. Our family and the love that holds my heart in place. The song on the radio ends. Adverts.

I clamber back into the bedroom holding onto all my body – shivering numb. My mouth feeling as dry as the city's moon. The air puts away its knives. Shaking. I run over to my wailing baby knowing all I'll ever love will grow to outlive me.

Building Six

There are those among us who have managed to forge a certain kind of contentment out of the whimsical temperament of life, a private sort of treasure accompanied by a long and nestled sleep. That was the first topic of conversation on that particular morning; sleep. Usually, I would have a new question for each day. That's how I liked to keep it back then. He would stress you can tell a lot about a person by the speed in which they can fall asleep. Not a half-sleep, but a real dead-state of unconsciousness. When I asked how long it took him to find that kind of slumber he fixed his gaze on me for what grew to be a discomforting amount of time – as if he half-expected me to already know the answer. He always did that, prolonged his response to something which didn't take his immediate fancy, or instead of trying to at least truncate his reply he would prefer to let the silence sit awkwardly between us both, while he culled a more precise language from somewhere inside that aberrant demeanour of his. Then at other times there was no answer. That's what found us on that November morning – he didn't answer at all.

Unlike him, I was rockingly impatient in those days, loaded with an attitude that lacked the patience for his esoteric games, so with a slight hesitance I pitched my question again, how long does it take you to fall sleep at night? He paused, blank-faced. A wide look that seemed to be noticing everything apart from me, then in a bewildered tone he asked me to repeat what I had just said. Now, I should state here that we'd both been awake since around 5am. For the next month our shift was scheduled to start at 6am every morning, so adopting any kind of primary focus wasn't exactly easy during those inorganic hours. Regardless, his capacity to maintain attention, or centre himself around one specific thing was often alarmingly dismal even at the best of times. On occasions I would catch those vacuous eyes of his winding themselves up against the verticality of the building, gradually climbing to meet the high ceilings until at last they would fly clear out of the double doors – as if orphaned and wild and belonging to nobody at all. When I asked him once why that tended to happen he said he wasn't exactly sure. Perhaps he suggested it was all the hours he'd spent watching doors that had instilled in him a kind of escape mechanism, a phantasmagorical hypnosis allowing him to make quite extraordinary things out of very ordinary situations. He often spoke like that. A fitting analogy I thought, one reserved for people like us.

People like us. What most fail to appreciate about the nature of security work is that you quickly develop a propensity to enlarge and dramatise even the smallest, most insignificant of happenings as they become the only things able to assuage the long tedium of standing and having to keep vigilant. Most of the workers leave the building at around 5pm. He and I stand by the door wishing people a good evening, smiling amicably while they scurry past us obliviously, holding up their ID passes to which we say thank you. Thank you. Thank you. Goodnight. Thank you sir. Goodnight madam. Goodnight. Thank you sir. Yesterday a group of office workers were too heavily engrossed in their conversation to remember the rules. As they walked past two of the men failed to show their ID's, they merely swiped the metallic strip along the card reader, automatically opening the barriers then unconcernedly strolled out the doors. They had to show us their ID's. It was mandatory. You had to show us before the swipe. He called out, excuse me. Softly at first, then with baritone authority. However their conversations seemed far more pressing, far more interesting than his command to halt. They waltzed through the doors letting out a mighty laugh presumably related to their conversation's subject. He shook his head in the way men do when they've reached the end – the end of everything that is somehow destined to last forever. For the rest of the shift he devoted himself to the walls, his facial expression burying itself in the mud of his mouth, his have a goodnight sinking down into the mute valleys of his throat.

Today was a new day yet I couldn't help but wonder if he was still hung up about all that. Just before I opened my mouth to bring it up he confessed he'd stopped listening to anything I was saying. He said I spoke too much in general. Nonchalantly he remarked how he could see the wending routes my mouth took whenever I asked my questions, the mime of redundant speech he called it, your lips knocking tirelessly against the doors of your crooked teeth, releasing words void of anything distinctively sufficient. That's how he phrased it. He always said things in that way, verbosely crushing without shame. Another thing I noticed over the short time we worked together was how there always appeared to be a discernible lapse of concentration revealing itself moments before his attention would become lost completely. His eyes would dart off like a set of gambler's dice being thrown into a corner of his mind, a place I liked to believe was capable of offering him some kind of solace; a world he felt lucky to be alive in perhaps. A space lambent with living hearts that had come to beat just for him. A place to feel a little important in as everyone likes to every once in a while. I can't remember exactly when but I did ask him once what it was like having such a terrible attention span. He said it felt easy, with an emphasis on the words *light* and *uncomplicated*. I stayed thinking about that for some time while the day trudged absently through us.

On another occasion I asked him how he dealt with the latent banality which establishes itself when working on the door. The reason I asked was partly because I myself always found the boredom overtly torturous and also because he looked to be at relative peace with the pointlessness of such a position. You're probably thinking I'm mad, or I'm slightly in love with him or something, but I'm not. It's just in those days he was the most fascinating man I'd ever met. My imagination he would declare shiningly. That's where it all goes. A place only he alone could access. His imagination. His sanctum. A realm he could fall into when he decided it was time to conjure up his mind's lucid medicine. He would often say he was making notes. Writing with the pen of his eye. Writing. I didn't know people still did that kind of thing. Kept notebooks and diaries and such. We weren't allowed to use pens or to even write things down on the door, unless it was related to a specific incident, so instead he would internalise everything – writing with the pen of his eye. It was a way for him to be whoever he wanted to be. Through writing he could win any battle, he could have any woman he wished or be the most important person left on earth. He was a fantasist. I didn't know that then, but I do now. Whenever I tell people about him the first thing they say to me is he sounds like a right weirdo. They don't even have the decency to pick another word for him. A dreamer they might stretch to say yet he was so much more. More than any of them would ever amount to, but then again how were they supposed to know. Those are the real tragedies, when greatness gets murdered by the long invisibility we ourselves create. Thinking about it now, he could do this thing where he would blur the lines between fiction and fact, to the point I myself wasn't sure who he was or if anything he ever told me was true. He once referred to himself as a child of colour and mind. It resonated in such a way I had to write it down come lunchtime on some tissue. That same afternoon he saw me scribbling something else he had just said, leaning into my ear he murmured words along the lines of you should never be scared to write anything down mate, even if you don't understand it at the time, grab it in its abstraction. Writing should always be the last thing you fear.

But now back to the question at hand, the one about sleep. One would assume that anybody who asked you to repeat at 6.30am something as basic as how long does it take you to fall asleep at night would follow it up with some kind of apology. Etiquette. That's what any dignified person would do, but not him. On this morning, while we stood waiting to receive the usual throng of corporate workers with my question still unanswered, he seemed more introverted than usual. I mean, he was never the most convivial of characters but you wouldn't exactly label him hermetical either. He seemed contemplative. Maybe he hadn't slept well. Maybe he'd been arguing with his girlfriend, or maybe he didn't have a girlfriend, but then if he did she couldn't have been that important because he never spoke about her, or perhaps she was so important he couldn't bring himself to share her brilliance with someone like me. Those were the kind of thoughts I was having back then, before now. With hindsight, all these particular intricacies seemed to act as the perfect segue into what was about to unfold.

An employee from the 4th floor had forgotten her pass. She worked for a finance company called GDS. This sort of thing was a usual occurrence, but what was about to happen was one of those incidences you couldn't just brush off after a beer and a cold shower. Due to this quite unfortunate staff member arriving with no official identification we weren't permitted to let her into the building, despite the fact we both saw her repeatedly on the mornings we were on guard. We knew her face well enough to have been able to grant her the benefit of the doubt if we found it in us to do so. I even remembered her names, both of them, but I didn't tell him. He was firm. Possibly angry about something as I said, standing there like a roguish general yet still managing to look correct. A thin looking scar trailing just above his right ear proved he could survive altercations if he had to. She was short. Maybe she was in her late twenties or early thirties. I wasn't sure. She had neat black hair that appeared conservative yet sophisticated suggesting she most probably valued who she was in life. Her position. Her job. The face she met in the mirror each morning. Maybe. Her mouth had a certain weight which gripped both the edges. She wore a standard red lipstick as was common with the women of Building Six, along with what appeared to be a freshly applied coat of lipgloss. This addition gave those sections of her poor smile a sort of positive, bright sheen, yet what struck me most about her was the sharp authority in her left eye. I don't know how else to describe it. That one observation continued to speed around my mind vertiginously – a sharp authority in the left eye.

Prior to this she would walk past us each morning with a cup of fresh coffee in one hand and her mobile phone in the other, thumbing over the screen or speaking confidentially to someone. She hardly ever looked up to notice our faces. Her pass always remained fixed onto her suit jacket, a small plastic ID card clipped neatly onto the pocket just above her hip. Rupal Shah. That was the name printed in bold capital letters just under the discoloured passport-size photo which made a disastrous attempt at trying to resemble her. She looked much better outside the photo, then again, most people always do.

On this particular day he looked at her in the same way he looked at me after I had asked about his sleeping tendencies. The question he still hadn't answered. In a low, frank tone he said Madam, I need to see your ID. Usually such assertions would begin with the word sorry or excuse me but today he omitted all that before proceeding to notify her for the second time that her pass wasn't visible. In startled disbelief she hastily knelt down placing the coffee-cup on the floor. Her mobile phone gripped tightly by the right hand, the one which proudly showcased her wedding ring. I noticed streaks of finger sweat begin to spread over the black screen, probably from panic.

Now he and I were the guardians at the royal gates, the heroic voices besieged by the walls and she was stood there bringing us to life in a blind cruelty; endowing us with function and purpose in the exact way a cheap garden slug relies desperately on the prosperous array of plants and earth in order to recognise its own putrid carrion. Even if that means its only function in life is to absorb the dark ridicule of being subjected to crawling and slithering across every colour, every shape and shade the earth had delicately invented. And he hated her for it.

She looked up at us both. Stones lodged between her scintillating eyes. No. He didn't let her through. He remained adamant he needed to see some kind of official identification. We were a nuisance. Seething through her clenched teeth with red lipstick burning, her voice scaling higher. Incredulous. Bringing round the handbag that fashioned her shoulder she began to briskly rummage through its mixed contents. I spotted a half-empty packet of travel tissues. What I presumed was a make-up bag. An assortment of pills. Energy tablets. A white phone charger. A baby's dummy. A few old chocolate wrappers torn down the middle. But no pass.

She swore. Once into her bag then twice into the air when the realisation properly took hold. One that made it clear that at 9.13am on a cold Thursday morning, she would have to make a pointless commute back home to retrieve her pass. An inconvenience induced by the two stupid men who stood in front of her. Men who simply wouldn't let her walk into the same building she'd been walking into for over two years, long before they both happened to be standing there checking ID's for a living in suits far less impressive than hers, and for a wage far more comical. When she felt the sobering reality working itself against the several sips of coffee she'd had prior to this encumbrance her shoulders fell loosely back. Her head tilted up towards the ceiling while she simultaneously bit down on her paper-white teeth, causing the lower contours of her jaw-muscles to push out the side of her face, to the point I could see them announce themselves in that delicate beauty of hers – like some kind of special guest at a gala full of dull and haggard people. She found both our faces looking at her plain and languid adding to the indignation we'd both burdened her with.

She swore again, only this time it was loud and direct, a magnificently executed monosyllabic word in its plural form – cunts. Vociferously she expelled all her pent-up vehemence steering it to land directly in the centre of our ocean-blue security badges, right inside the heart of our names. My eyes shamefully pitted themselves against the heels of my shoes while his face remained unabashed by the jagged tirade of her profanity. His eyes were fixed and sure in their attempt not to get swept away by the salty waters beginning to engulf hers. That handsome expression of his remaining unspoilt. Rupal Shah so obviously had failed to understand this was his stadium. Not mine. Or hers. Or the Prime Minster's or God's. But his. And right now he was the only person who needed to be here. The light recognised him and him alone; as if this was the anticipated come-on he'd been waiting for his entire life. I marvelled at the spectacle and indeed a spectacle it was. That was the job. To close your eyes to names and faces of people who were so obviously familiar. To remove yourself from any possibility of making someone's day that little less stressful.

Her tone changed again. She was softer now, affirming with both hands clasped that we knew her, maybe not by name but definitely by face. She was sure of it. Ever since she returned from maternity leave we had greeted her with a hello or a good morning. That I even ran after her to hand back the shawl she dropped the other week, but all this changing of method and technique proved futile. He was unyielding, obstinate in his role as security guard of Building Six. The lightness in her voice began to ebb away, almost as if admitting to itself that all other alternatives were now rendered ineffective, like the final moments a doctor steps in to inform a family their loved one has only moments left to live. The workers by now would be neatly tucked behind their desks, huddled in their meeting rooms with cups of warm tea and coffee or babbling away on phones and responding to emails, while the three of us stood there in our bizarre showdown, impervious to sympathy and shame.

Then I saw it. Right there in an instant. The first sign of weakness from Rupal Shah. A small pearl of a tear broke out from the corner of her left eye, the same eye that previously had looked at us with such sharp authority, but was now rapidly becoming something else. It looked hot and lonely, sunken and defeated rolling over the both of us as we stood head-on to face the calamity. I glanced over to him in what must have looked like a superficial attempt to seek some type of guidance, something of a proposition as to what we should be doing in a situation such as this. Nothing. He positioned his feet so as to have them slightly apart, placed one hand over the other allowing them to rest authoritatively in front of him. I recall thinking amidst such a tense and uncomfortable situation that these tears of Rupal Shah's seemed to resemble a community of small rocks all tumbling down the body of a giant volcano. In this context he was the volcano or maybe the situation might have been, I hadn't really decided, I couldn't, I had a job to be getting on with.

Despite trying to not notice the direction of her tears I couldn't help but watch them move as if they were free to travel any part of her face, without restriction, without needing to identity themselves to anyone. I thought about that while he continued the very painstaking, almost clinical shake of his head – the proverbial mast of rejection, the never-ending insolence we both knew so well. No. No. No. I do this thing. I still do, even after all this time. I always look at a person's ears when they move their head repeatedly, especially when those moments are born out of sticky confrontation. No. No. No. There's something very infantile about ears, something unthreatening and helpless. Watching his just cling to the side of his head like that despite his skewed scar seemed almost as intriguing as the list of quaint crystals which by now were running uncontrollably down the side of Rupal Shah's face, clashing with all the confidence of her glossed lips, adding a new kind of grief to the bright red which was so sure of itself a mere ten minutes ago.

In a desperate blubber of unmanageable sound she demanded to see the building site-manager. All the emotion, all the swearing and pleading hadn't worked, so as a final resort the idea was to now get bureaucratic. The manager was a man named Keith O'Conner, or Con as we called him. I pulled out the walkie-talkie, turned up the little black dial and radioed in. Within minutes the lift door opened with its usual symphonic glide to reveal Keith, a hefty man who was paid far more than any of us to drink worrying amounts of coffee while watching the CCTV screens from the spy-dens of the main security office, and occasionally yell orders down the radio if guards appeared to be slouching or distracted. Approaching us he was all stomach and keys. Clipped onto his waist the fat set jangled and clinked as if in parody of the musical dissonance one might expect from an office building security manager. As the three of us stood there, Rupal Shah began to relay her side of the story. How she had left the house in a frenzied rush to catch her train. How she's having a really tough time at the moment with her husband, how the meeting she'd spent the last few weeks scheduling had started ten minutes ago, a meeting with a group of willing investors from China that she's now most definitely missed. She stressed how we both knew her; how we saw her on the mornings we worked. She even included the story of the shawl, which did touch me, although I would never bring myself to show it.

Keith, turning down the volume to his walkie-talkie listened attentively. He had a fantastic listening face. Sincerely contorted, with perfectly assured head-nods automatically appearing after each narrative sentence fell from the lips of the very animated Rupal Shah. He however remained as voiceless as the polished shoes we stood in. He knew the rules too well. Keith, with his professional mannerism, let her finish speaking, until suggesting she should try to call her boss and see if he could perhaps grant her the permission required to pass through. Her face rediscovered itself. Her last lifeline. She took out her phone making a few shuffling steps away from where we stood. Exchanging a hushed combination of short words with the person on the other end she removed the device from her ear returning to her irremediably sad expression. 'He's not in the office. The secretary just told me he's out having meetings all day.' That was it. Done. Nobody else had the authority to bypass security regulations. If silence wanted a corporeality of its own then it would have been fine to appropriate the one we were now all embodied in. It was uncomfortable seeing her standing there so desolate. Suddenly I was struck by the thought to sign her in as a visitor, that way we could curtail the regulations, then that too would have been of little use as she had already made it known to everyone that she was an employee of GDS. There were no other permissible ways for Rupal Shah to enter. She was going to have to go home.

All this was stipulated procedure documented in the Building Six security handbook. We'd all undergone a mandatory day of training aimed at preparing us for situations such as this. I still have the handbook somewhere. Keith looked on while calmly roving three chunky fingers around the edges of his chin, rubbing as if he were the one trying to edge himself back into a state of comprehension. With a very gentle clearing of the throat he could do nothing besides confirm that his colleagues were in fact right, that the defeated Rupal Shah, with her exposed quarry of drying crystal tears, would have to venture back home if she wanted to be let into Building Six. ID cards were a strict requirement. Obligatory. There were to be no exceptions. All this sat in accordance with the direct orders decreed by Mr. Cohen himself – he was the property tycoon who owned the entire building.

Catching a glimpse of her apparent despair Keith went on to affectionately retell an incident involving a man who was let into the building with no official ID back in March. He told how this intruder turned out to be the crazed husband of a woman who'd been subjected to extreme bouts of domestic violence at the hands of the aforementioned. I could see how her eyes immediately started to focus in on the story. Keith knew he wasn't really allowed to elaborate any more. I remember thinking to myself he'd already said slightly too much. Still, he was the boss, he had more authority than us ordinary guards and so he went on. This maniacal husband had connivingly told the security on the door that his wife was diabetic and had forgotten her insulin. He claimed emphatically it was no joke and there was no time for second thoughts. The guard on the door had only been working for two weeks. Naturally he was inexperienced at knowing how to tell the phony from the sincere, so he let the scumbag straight through with a set of assisting directions mapping out the quickest way to get to the floor the poor woman was working on. It was all caught on camera by Paul who was working the CCTV upstairs. We heard later on how earlier that morning her husband had found out she was having an affair, and so had really only come to Building Six with the scandalous intention of shaming her up in front of the entire office then probably beating her when she got home. The police weren't called but we sent the recordings over to them anyway as things of that nature had to be officially reported and logged. We heard how the incident even made its way into the local papers. Since that unfortunate day Mr. Cohen specifically stated any staff without the proper forms of identification must be refused entry, irrespective of status or company. Keith apologised. Tilted his head to one commiserative side and let his mouth force a smile for both his fat cheeks. I don't know how much of the anecdote registered with Rupal Shah, but what I did know was how her head shook itself in slow and painful disbelief.

Keith left us to face what our dogged application of building law had cast upon the morning of Rupal Shah. There was no more coffee; that was definitely cold. Her phone was now lying useless and abandoned somewhere inside her handbag, mascara smeared like a melted night around her eyes. I could see she may have been a lot younger than I originally had presumed. People always look younger after they've been able to cry properly. He was standing looking beyond Rupal Shah. Maybe out of culpability but more likely out of indifference. The door's electric slide received the final herd of panicked late workers. A cold burst of wind hit the three of us, entering the building wrapped in its traditional November skin only to be tackled by the entrance heater as it ran into the path of its small blowing. The fan working indefatigably from the top of the door. She regained her composure. accepting the inalienable truth that she would have to make another tiresome commute back home just to fetch a totally irrelevant ID badge to access a building she'd been working in for over two years. An ID card so irrelevant in the grand scheme of things it may as well have not been issued at all. Pointless. To put it in perspective, once the day drew to an end, she and all the other two thousand odd people working within Building Six would forget their passes in places where mystery itself wouldn't even care to acknowledge. Pointless. These two stupid, inconveniencing little men with their pathetic plastic badges and their soulless, hysterical, brainless jobs which a bloody traffic-cone could probably do better have purposefully become the root to all this totally unnecessary aggravation. This is what Rupal Shah's brain was most likely contending with during the moments leading up to her saying this.

'I have a baby who's nine months old at home with the only friend I have left in the world. I've a husband who shows me the insides of his own hell every night, and the only man who could have saved me from it all is dead. I come to work each day, to an office which reeks of cheap furniture polish, coffee, bad breath and the latest duty-free perfumes but I've learnt to keep my problems to myself. I want to work hard and get the promotion I need, the one to make everything alright again, for me and my little son.'

Pausing, she blew her nose into the penultimate tissue she'd unraveled from her thin and crumpled travel-pack.

'Can I ask, do you have children?' She asked him with all seriousness. He didn't answer. He just kept looking straight ahead at the door. Then she asked me the same question. I replied bashfully that I didn't. I also said her story sounded sad and I was sorry for the type of morning she was having. In response she smiled with the only smile she had left, one that happened in only half her mouth while trying to frantically wipe away the crusty lace of tears which by now had desecrated the triumph of her beauty. She must have known if he weren't there I would have let her pass. I think that hurt her more than anything else. Moving closer to him, brimming with venom and war, like a tank monstrously sizing up some remote village house and with the muscles in her face recoiling to form their initial defensive bastion she said scornfully, 'I don't think you have a wife. In fact I don't think you have anyone you really love. You take this thing you do so seriously you can't see what your pathetic hang-ups do to people. You're on a power trip, you all are, because you know the moment you step outside this building and that square you stand on gets taken back by whoever owns you, you're reminded how insignificant …'

She stopped there. Maybe because she was now looking at me or maybe for another reason. She wore the tenuous expression of someone who was hurting more than the person they were trying to hurt. Her invective onslaught running out of the hate needed to sustain it. Neither of us took offence. I kept looking straight ahead in the same way he was doing. Professional. Unaffected. Authoritative. All he cared to say was when you have your ID you'll be able to pass with no hassle. Inferably she nodded, followed by an exhausted sigh. Turning her back, she took two steps towards the door then turned to face us. I knew she would. She had too much to say, she could have spent hours talking about the people who had let her down, which for us would have been fine, seeing as we were both standing inside all the time we would ever own. We were non-entities in the multifaceted ranks of life and status and maybe she felt safe in that knowledge – we didn't really exist as real people who anyone should take or did take too seriously. That particular thought upset me. Why was she telling us all this? What she really seemed to want to do was tell us the story of her eyes. Both of them. It's what most sad people yearn for. To let strangers into the tumultuous world they inhabit alone behind the giant facade.

'I'm sorry. I didn't mean for all that to come out. It's just been a very difficult time for me. I'm sorry.' She stopped to dig awkwardly at her clear nails, picking away at the cuticles until saying, 'do you have a name?' He didn't reply. His face hadn't moved throughout the whole period she stood there, scolding and degrading us, so she turned to me.

'Can you tell me your friend's name?'

'Alex,' I said, 'his name's Alex.'

'Thank you. I'm Rupal, I work on the fourth floor for a finance company called GDS.'

Everything was changing again, new characters, a turn in the plot, new ways to manipulate and bully by utilising a different set of emotions to evoke a more profound sense of guilt. She sounded younger, like a lost teenaged girl asking for directions in the hard-lands of a foreign city. 'Alex, what do you do when you're not at work?' That was when I felt sorry for him. I wanted her to leave him alone now. I wanted to tell her to stop, but I didn't. She was gaining traction, working her way into the same place I myself had wanted for so long to go, a place I was denied by the fear I had of being too intrusive. She was drilling, rumbling his walls, aiming for the opaque shields he kept staunchly intact. This was the part of him that lay lightless and undiscovered, invisible in its own obscurity. Rupal Shah was standing at the doors of his most famous mystery, a place where ID badges were as useful as keys are to a cave.

'Do you have a hobby Alex? Do you like football, cars, weight training?' Her tone slightly mellowed into a dallying probe with fluttering intonations. She had reversed what should normally be happening in a situation such as this. Usually one would expect hints of patronisation from the victim, from the person wronged, but her questioning seemed to flow in a more cordial way. Maybe it was the crystals that still lingered around her face, maybe it was the story she shared or maybe I was adding my own hints of piteous idealism to the situation. Either way she hadn't morphed into the type of person that would reinforce the reasons why he took so much pleasure in denying people entry into the building, although he said before they all had it in them. To talk to us like we didn't exist. Like we didn't matter. To say what they pleased. Here Rupal Shah was showing a new kind of initiative, one that left him facing the skinned heart of his own emptiness.

Then she said, 'This may sound a little strange but what the hell, do you have a garden?' Silence. Both of us. Silence. She continued, 'You know gardens can teach you a lot about things that like to stay quiet. We have a garden behind the flat, nothing special really, but my son seems to enjoy the hours we spend back there. When I was on maternity leave he would sit in his pushchair looking straight at all the colours. My husband's a gardener. We bought the flat because of the little plot of land. One section is his, the other mine. It's something quite beautiful to watch, the way all those wild things bloom from nothing, from just a tiny seed, small and insignificant enough to get washed down a bathroom sink but big enough to fit into the whole world.' Her face became a fairground, each element enjoying its own particular ride and sensation; she was travelling now and had us with her. 'How can such natural life happen so quietly and perfectly around us, without anyone stopping to notice its virtue? During that summer I saw things you would never have known existed. I built something sacred. I mean, I still don't know all the names of the flowers, the families they come from, but that doesn't bother me. Each one seemed happy just being acknowledged. Just being marvelled at by some stranger. Every single shape satisfied to be held up by some kind of light. The more you start to notice these things the more they all begin to grow in your direction. If only life could be as simple as a garden, right?'

I gestured only with my head trying hard not to seem too interested in what she was saying. I wanted her to leave, but then I wanted her to stay forever too. His face still anchored to the robotic doors up front. The receptionists at the main desk could be heard talking and taking messages on the phone. The postman cut past us, the smell of the outside tattooed onto the fabric of his red winter coat. City pigeons could be seen pecking at stale crumbs, their plumage the same colour as exhaust fumes. It was business as usual, everything stuck in the artifice of its time.

'As a young girl I spent years trying to find a way I could define myself. I wasn't happy being just a woman, just a daughter, and then eventually having to become someone's wife and mother. I felt there was so much more to me than just that. I had things, qualities nobody cared to notice because of who I appeared to be; my looks, my skin colour, my gender, the way I spoke or what God I believed in. In the corporate world you see how people deal with their preconceptions. How hard it is to become bigger than your stereotype. Recently I started to notice the way flowers grew. They had no real idea they were flowers, it's a name we've given them. They didn't feel the need to define themselves in the ways we do. They held no prejudices, there was no violence encaged within them, no jealousy or malevolence. All they needed to know was they could keep growing towards the light. That was it. Just grow towards the light.'

Snapping my badge up I rushed to swipe it across the barrier so as she could pass but his hand was already on my wrist, pressing down tightly, leaving four white lanes on the surface of my skin just above the veins; his eyes an ancient mausoleum inside mine. My pass fell back. I cowered, hating him more than ever. I wanted her to rip him apart. To tear out his heart just to prove he had one, but she didn't, she never could. She was too grand a vessel in a world ambushed and flooded by misery and fear.

'No please, don't worry, it's fine. I'm going to head home anyway. I've taken up too much of your time as it is, plus I know you're both just doing your jobs. It's out of character for me to act like this. On the plus side though at least I won't have to worry about intruders forging their way in here. I've missed my meeting now anyway. Maybe I'll just take the rest of the day off. Jesus, look at me, what a disaster.' She turned to face the outside, away from us.

'It's brightened up hasn't it?' She checked the time on her phone. 'Maybe I'll go get my son and take him to sit in the garden for a while.'

The crystals had all vanished leaving a flurry of faint streaks like infant chemtrails over the sky of her face. She rubbed at them with the last clean tissue in her bag, disposing of the one she used previously in the empty packet then picking up her cold coffee-cup. Indeed she was right; the day had brightened up. The sun was out to discover our doors. It was approaching 10am, time for our first tea break. A spectacular shaft of clean daylight bounced through the windows of Building Six, illuminating our polished section of stone marble flooring. The plastic plants placed either side of us appearing to be happy in the their infamy. Walking straight through the doors, we both watched the way they gracefully slid to open, granting Rupal Shah access to a world we had no control over and no voice in. Fast and synchronised they parted. Like two dancers perfectly tuned in to the weeping belt of a singular act. From a few feet away she looked back on us; standing beneath the door's sensors so as to prevent them from closing and reopening, like they understood something about the relevance of what she was about to confess, obsequiously allowing her to deliver these final few words.

'I haven't had a good night's sleep in two years, since around the time I got married. He can be the cruelest of animals at the most desperate of times. What makes it all increasingly harder to bear is our neighbours too can't decide whether they should be loving or hating each other. It was only the other night when the guy who lives in the flat above ours, who I've never actually spoken to or seen, surprised me. You can usually hear all the screaming and fighting between him and his partner. The other night was different. There was no fighting. Instead, he was speaking something out loud, words to himself perhaps, or maybe to her. Some of it sounding too muffled for me to understand, but by the way he was saying everything a strange sense of peace came over me, one I haven't been able to feel in years. That night I slept so deep I have no recollection of me even climbing into bed, plus, my husband he didn't come home either which I know helped. I hear the guy leave for work in the early hours each morning, but I can't say I've ever see him come home. From the sounds of it I don't think he gets much sleep.'

I looked over at him. He hadn't moved. Frozen in his ridiculous security pose. The doors gallantly rejoined. Standing exhausted inside myself I watched Rupal Shah make her way into the big future while he allowed himself to stand naked and beaten at the doors of his crammed suffering. Those hopeless crystals. How splendidly they erupted over his entire mouth conquering everything he'd tried so diligently to guard. An entire sky of white gold planting a million wet stars all over his great wretchedness. Over his badge they fell exploding. Over his muted words. His stubborn reticence. His tangled dreams and nightmares. Over his fragility. His pride. His jacket and shoes. The ones that kept him so firmly positioned in those twelve-hour shifts. His athletic posture cancelling itself out, giving way to the indelible resplendency of all his muzzled agony. The scar on the side of his head still lurid and alive. I didn't ask him if he was alright. The questions had exceeded themselves already today, plus I already got my answer. I checked my watch, it was 10.18am, time for a break I thought and yet nothing had even happened.

Have You Ever Seen A Big Man Fall?

I t was a song they all liked so Paul turned the radio up. When it finished Little Terry turned it back down so as to avoid hearing the irritating adverts. That's when he collapsed. Hussein. It took both Paul and Little Terry to try and lift him back up. Rushing. Paul grabbed Hussein from under his right armpit, his face vasodilating under the immense strain of the effort, while Little Terry, being little, remained unable to handle the side of Hussein weighing the most. The side where his heart lived. Distressed, he called out to Massimo who was the only other person in the room. Panicking, Paul yelled at him to come over and give Little Terry a hand with his side. Rather than complying, Massimo seemed more inclined to want to know what had just happened. Paul retorted aggressively telling him to shut up, to help with the lift, then bring a chair over to sit him in. Massimo subsequently fell into a state of confusion; what was he to do first? The chair or the lift?

Little Terry yelled for the second time how he couldn't lift Hussein alone, he needed assistance. Hussein was out. Cold. Someone suggested to call Con, the building site manager and pandemonium ensued. The voice sounded like Massimo's who, despite there being one right in front of him, was still looking all over for a chair. Going against what Paul had initially ordered he reasoned that the chair should take precedence over the assisting lift. Once the chair was in place he could then help Little Terry and Paul mount the giant Hussein up onto it. What would be the use in lifting up such a man then having nowhere to sit him? That was his logic. So amidst the heat and turbulence of the dreaded moment he decided the first thing anyone should ever do if they happen to encounter a big man falling, is to look for a place to sit them. Somewhere secure and supportive. Massimo's thinking however was soon rendered useless when circumstance would prove that a chair, in this context, would be totally ineffective. He wasn't to come to this realisation until after he had hurriedly wheeled the seat over to where Hussein lay. How are we supposed to get him on there if he's unconscious? Said one of the two men. What kind of idiot are you Mass? Profanity ensued. Arguing. Insults. Then came the speculations. The cause of the collapse. Paul said Hussein was feeling unwell that morning. He'd wondered why he wasn't saying much. He seemed slightly under the weather. Little Terry just kept repeating the words heart attack. If we manage to get him on the chair we can at least check to see if he's still breathing. This was said by Massimo who had at last brought himself around to help lift the side which held Hussein's heart. The side too heavy for Little Terry to lift alone. We can see if he's still breathing while he's on the floor said Paul. Have any of you lot done first aid? The answer was a collective and disappointing no. Ok, after three we're going to lift him up onto the seat. It was clear who'd given that order. The three men slowly raised big Hussein up onto the wheeled chair. Six foot three inches and fifteen stone of unconscious man. The only other person who had ever seen him in such a helpless way was his mother twenty-eight years ago, and his wife. Get him water quick. Now, check his breathing. Well? Feel for a pulse then. He's dead! He's fucking dead! No, that's the wrong side you idiot. Put a mirror under his nose. I don't have a bloody mirror. Then use something else for fuck sake. Like what? I don't fucking know do I? What am I, a bloody paramedic? Shut up you twat! Both of you shut up, look, use the screen of your watch. I can see mist. He's alive. Thank fuck.

Massimo ran over to the monitor which surveyed the main doors. He could see Con talking to a lady and two security guards. He radioed in. Con's walkie-talkie was clipped onto his belt. It must be turned down. Forget Con. That was Little Terry who said that, going on to call Hussein's name repeatedly. Loudly. In his ear. As if Hussein had just walked out the door and had left his keys behind. Paul took the water that Little Terry had brought over, splashing it anxiously over those unresponsive parts of Hussein's face. Eyes. Movement. Life. Then, slowly, he regained form. His body developing itself into the holds of the chair supplied by Massimo, losing the support of the two men who were inflexibly positioned either side of him.

What happened mate, you scared the living shit out of us? Little Terry said. You alright Huss, can you breathe? Mass, go grab him some more water will you, said Paul.

Massimo filled a bottle from the drinking tap outside the room. Hussein rubbed his neck in a daze. He mentioned his head hurt. Maybe from the fall, maybe from something else. He didn't know what happened or how he blacked out like that. Paul asked him if he was diabetic. Hussein said he wasn't. Are you stressed asked Little Terry. I'm not sure. Perhaps. That's never happened to me before. The three men stood round him concerned and attentive listening as he spoke in a hacked, discombobulated tone. All I remember is the song on the radio had just finished then nothing, I was out. Yeah I know, I went over to turn it down then bang. My chair rumbled like we were in the middle of an earthquake or something. I looked around, saw you flat out on your face. I don't think I've ever seen a geeza fall like that before said Little Terry. Me neither said Paul. Massimo didn't say anything, instead he remained concernedly looking over at his colleague. Hussein took a small sip of the water then said again his head and neck hurt really bad. For the first time since all the commotion Massimo, with an unusual air of confidence and expertise, cleared his throat to say you might have concussion mate. Your best bet is to go hospital and get yourself looked at, better to be safe than sorry.

I think I should call my wife said Hussein. Little Terry looked over at Paul in the way a person might when a friend has just confessed they're dying inside and need desperately to talk to the person who's killing their heart. Turning away Paul shook his head, signalling to Little Terry it would be best to not say anything and let Hussein do what he needs to do. He understood. I'll make you a tea he said. The DJ on the radio could be heard plugging a gig for a band nobody knew. Massimo looked again at the CCTV screen which surveyed the main doors. Con was gone.

Hussein knew his wife would be at work. Mobile phones weren't permitted in the surveillance room as they were known to interfere with equipment, only a radio was allowed. Here you go pal. Little Terry brought him over a cup of hot tea, putting it down on the desk beside him. How you feeling now? Yeah a bit better, thanks boys. I'm really sorry to just drop on you like that. Don't be silly Huss, we're just glad it's nothing serious. I mean, it would have been a real nightmare if we had to carry you over to those lifts said Paul facetiously. Little Terry laughed. Massimo didn't. Instead he remarked by saying that little hobbit Terry couldn't even lift you so I don't know what he's bloody laughing at. I had to come over and help him put you on the chair. Fuck off you wobbly mug, yes I could, I just couldn't get a proper grip that's all. Anyway, what the fuck were you supposed to be doing? You brought a chair over for a bloke who was unconscious. What's he supposed to do with that, sit up and have his dinner? No wonder you're in here watching these screens six days a week… fucking retard! I brought a chair over because Paul told me to and anyway…Alright you two pack it in. Hussein's alright now so no need to start pouring your hearts out to each other. Someone try calling Con again. I just did Massimo said sulkily but he weren't answering, he must have the volume turned down on his walkie. What kind of manager fucks-off during moments like those anyway.

Another song came on the radio. Nobody recognised it. Massimo went back over to his unit as did Little Terry. Paul wiped away the circles of water left by the bottle. Hussein told Paul he was going outside to try and make a phone-call to his wife. Yeah no problem mate, take the afternoon off if you want and go get some rest. He took the lift down to the ground floor, heading for the back doors where the guards were permitted to smoke and make calls if necessary.

Outside the day was cold but bright. November. Taking his phone out from inside his blazer he unlocked the keypad to reveal the wallpaper picture he had on the screen, the one of him holding up his young daughter while she laughed playfully on his shoulders. His wife had taken the picture. He looked at it, once with his eyes, then again with his heart. The sky appeared to look as if it had just swallowed the entire sun. It wasn't bright anymore. Lifting his eyes from the screen he put the phone back into his pocket, then after a few seconds the giant Hussein headed back up to work.

Yellow Daffodil

The jury unanimously found Robert Shah guilty of murder in the first degree. The judge read out his sentence with the same metallic cadence he secretly reserved for such tragic cases. A pillowed murmur could be heard trying to conceal itself from somewhere in the back of the dreary room. While the judge spoke of the severity and brutishness of his actions, Robert Shah turned to catch sight of his mother-in-law burying her face into the cages of her weak interlocked fingers. The arms of her brother wrapped themselves around her shoulders as they convulsed synchronistically inside the relief of such a long awaited verdict. Their eyes caught halfway between a place of inconsolable indignation and of deep loss. The inscrutable expression holding together Robert Shah's face remained as unaffected as the day he first saw his father break his mother's jaw. As the day his older cousin tied him to a chair to ram a hot iron into his thigh, for fun. As the day his mother's new boyfriend crept into his room, accompanied by the spirited stench of cheap whiskey and tobacco-ash, to manoeuvre a sticky hand slowly, pantingly down into the bareness of his underwear. The day after his eighth birthday. The day which would subsequently crystallise the rest of his childhood, thrusting him into a tortured state of adolescence and adulthood. His famed stoicism could be seen compounded and unrelenting by the entire courtroom. When the judge asked if he had anything he wished to add before being removed from general society he nonchalantly declined. Two hefty guards stepped forward to usher him out of the room, a set of steel cuffs jangling on his limp wrists. The courtroom was adjourned. Conversations could be heard slowly emanating. Reflections on the case were openly shared by those involved since Sam Anderson's discovery of Rupal Shah's body on her kitchen floor – their baby wailing relentlessly until the neighbours concluded something must be terribly wrong.

The autopsy revealed she'd been stabbed eight times. Her face, after the ruthless sanguinary beating, showed multiple bruising in the tissue under the skin from what appeared to be previous assaults. The couple living above the Shah's home testified that her screams were never heard, suggesting she must have endured all her husband's cruelty in silence. The only audible sound on the night of the murder was the irregular throwing of what sounded like objects against a wall, followed by the final thump of something, or in this case someone, landing hard.

Within the following days Robert Shah was moved to a maximum security prison. There he would sit and recall the twenty-eight years which constituted all his life's experiences. Twenty-three hours each day would be spent rewinding segments his memory wouldn't allow him to forget, those major incidences culminating in him having to spend the rest of his adult life inside a prison cell. He would think about the mental scars he'd wantonly acquired along with the warped psychosis automatically inherited when the ramifications of those indecencies inflicted on the innocent take affect. For long hours he would appear unperturbed, reflecting on the scathed elements of his past with the same tired indifference of an old detective constantly replaying the footage to a crime he knew he'd be unable to solve. Gradually, over time, he will begin to feel the life of his skin and bones break away and die. His heart losing belief in its strength to function. His face will grow ever more pallid, acquiring a residual diffidence born out of solitude and decay. The process happens like this; firstly the eyes become subverted, finding the edges of both cheekbones. Secondly the mouth becomes stiff and contorted from the solemn nature that inhabits one's continuing prostration. The same prostration which bestows itself upon the prisoner's need to express and communicate with others, reducing them to a motionless sack of blood and organs. Lastly, the cambered shoulders of the inmate pronounce themselves as having won the battle for dominance over the remainder of the spirit's weary hope. A definitive conquering, symbolising the immanency of the end. Shoulders are where those condemned for their wicked ways are forced to bear the tension and listlessness famously known for attaching itself on to men who have nothing to do but think about time, and all that exists to sing and gallop around it.

Prison life has an almost legendary habit of forcing even the most hardened of criminals to confront the part of themselves they may be most terrified of, the part which in many cases would have been responsible for their fatal incarceration. The endless hours of grief-filled rumination, the bottomless months of boredom all give imputes to those moments capable of filling the stomach with twisted, citric knives. Insanity huddles up against the mind as the prisoner chops his way through past situations, irremediable and permanent. This in time increases, worsening to create a whole new kind of terror. After the first cold and unprovoked assault by a group of fierce inmates has been survived. After sleep has been sufficiently thwarted and insomnia has become a regularity. After the discreet bouts of shuffled masturbation have lost their embarrassment. After the longing for a woman's touch and the smell of her skin have died. After the letters and visitors from the free world are of no more. After the first suicide attempt fails and a struggling conversation with a priest is followed by a much recommended study of the bible, with particular focus on Ecclesiastes 7:17, *'Do not be a fool–why die before your time?'* Or similarly Mark 3:28-29 *'Verily I say unto you, all sins shall be forgiven unto the sons of men, and blasphemies wherewith soever they shall blaspheme, but he that shall blaspheme against the Holy Ghost hath never forgiveness, but is in danger of eternal damnation.'*

After all this has happened, the steel bones of the prison

begin to scaffold the body of every prisoner contained within. But when one ordinary grey Monday afternoon three men came to sit opposite Robert Shah while he ate a meal of mashed potato, peas and boiled chicken, nothing could have conditioned him to withstand what was about to happen. There were no words. No warnings. There never is. The irregular clatter of cutlery filled the entire refectory. All around unhurried men took small feckless steps with white plastic trays held out in front of them, containing the rationed meals that appeared to be just as lifeless as their very consumers. The daily anecdotal cacophony of mouths eager to communicate while ravenously trying to appease their hunger could be heard over the afternoon's happenings. The three men didn't say anything to each other nor to Robert Shah. They ate unlike the other convicts, choosing instead to imitate him with the same torpor, partially looking up between gulps. All four shovelled food into the corners of their mouths, chewing in the same cyclic motion. In the eleven months Robert Shah had so far served inmates had only attacked him twice. Judging by the villainous composition and general brutality of this particular jail that was itself a result. In his cell he concluded both attacks were incited by men needing to show dominance. Both times he didn't feel the need to retaliate. He had nothing to prove and nothing necessarily to live for. If he were killed it would simply mean the inevitable would have been actioned ahead of its time. He knew the injuries incurred by these attacks were minor in comparison to those he witnessed happening to others. On both occasions he was discharged from the prison's infirmary after only a few hours and returned to his cell. Yet luck is named luck for a reason; within its context it will soon have to encounter the antithetical unlucky moment so as to exemplify its true definition. And so on that ordinary Monday afternoon, while Robert Shah was still scraping the last few peas off his plate, the three anonymous inmates discreetly manoeuvred a make-shift blade from the hands of one man into those of the allotted attacker. From under the table, away from the hungry mouths and eyes of the refectory, a single and expert blow swooped through the blind air known for infamously occupying the space beneath prison tables. Within seconds the crude weapon settled with tremendous agony inside the flesh of Robert Shah's right thigh. The one that coincidently still bore the obtrusive scar of a hot iron plate, compliments of his cousin and the games they would play. Instantly, he fell to the ground emitting an irrepressible scream. The blood flowed quick and efficiently, escaping his body, owning the floor, his hands and clothes. Holding onto the gash his vision focused on the refectory lights, slowly retracting into a deeper blur, until at last he became safely enclosed in the catacombs of his own blessed unconsciousness. The bedlam that followed around him allowed his attackers to merge stealthily back into the rising panic without fear of arrest or accusation.

He regained consciousness some time later having lost nearly six pints of blood. The prison doctors did their best to keep him breathing through the transparent tubes of a ventilator, which he did, albeit hoarsely and mechanically.

His leg was covered in a mesh of thick white bandages, patches of red blood seeping through sorely. It was then I spoke to him for the first time. He opened his eyes slightly. I was sitting up in bed reading the day's newspaper recovering from an operation I'd undergone last Thursday. Usually inmates weren't permitted to share the same ward but all other seclusion units were taken, so they'd put us in together, a warden keeping close watch by the door. His lips were dry. His eyes struggling to prove themselves to his face. He didn't speak, he couldn't, so seeing the moment to be opportune I decided to introduce myself.

'Alright mate? You had a bit of rough day? Yep, you did. You're one lucky bastard you know that? They almost got you right in the pride and jewels! The fella who got it fortnight ago weren't so lucky. Don't know if you heard about him.'

I turned another page then stopped to take a proper look at him, calamitous and mute. He began to blink with a panicked promptness, with the rapidity of a person who was no longer equipped with the ability to speak and shout, but who wanted desperately to express their complete shock and incredulity at their predicament. A hysterical, extensive blink stuck paralysed in the pools of his despair. He'd lost the ability to speak; a thick tube clinging to his cracked lips, crust and tape all around as he lay steeped in the stale uniform of the dead.

'Do you remember their faces? What they looked like?'

The whites of his eyes were a gone-off sunset, withdrawing themselves into the assailed banks of his memory. The three men. He only would have seen them once, maybe twice. He was down and hungry. He remembered the masticating sound in his head as he chomped through overly salted boiled chicken. He was trying to speak but life was still reorganising itself within. He remembered small insignificant details. White. Clean-shaven. Blue eyes. Tattoo on neck. St George's cross.

'Don't stress yourself mate. Relax. These are the kind of questions they're going to ask you in a few days that's all.' I couldn't bring myself to tell him that even if he knew their names, even if he knew the names of their mothers, wives and daughters, it wouldn't make a blind bit of difference. Prison is prison. The last stop for the forlorn and the wicked. If the men were caught where would they go? Solitary confinement? Maybe get a beating from the guards? This was the end of the line. Robert Shah was a renowned loner. He had nobody to help fight his wars and in prison that's the most dangerous position for an inmate to be in.

Despite all the confusion and the excruciating pain the other major concern facing Robert Shah would have been why. Why him? Why was he singled out? As he lay helplessly beneath the ceiling I could almost see his mind race, looking for a plausible explanation to help satisfy all the confusion. He was in prison for murder. He had taken the life of his wife. A defenceless and good woman. The mother of his only child. A woman he'd been introduced to by his parents and encouraged to marry. A marriage he was never fully complicit in. A marriage he was never fully happy in. One he grew to begrudge and could only really express that peculiar repugnance through the evils and cowardice of violence. A violence that for him felt natural and learnt. Could it have been a warranted attack by a group of men targeting prisoners who committed crimes of a seemingly gutless and less masculine nature? A group of men who saw it fit and righteous to attack and murder woman-beaters and pedophiles. Was there a covert vigilante group of staunch feminists perhaps? Surely most of the animals locked within these cages had at some point all turned their fists onto their women? Wasn't it part of their initiation? A prerequisite for credibility. The sacred axiom of the inner-city drug dealer. The petty thief. The corporate fraudster. The street robber, pervert and pimp. He didn't know where to begin.

Robert Shah was a monster, as were all the other men confined to the guilty verdict of their own unforgivable atrocity, but he wasn't made of typical inmate material. In some ways men like Robert Shah surpass the common sociopathy found in places such as this. He wasn't hard, fearless or inwardly psychotic insofar as I could tell. I had seen him around before, always alone, always withdrawn and dejected but never appearing to be a threat to anyone. In fact, given a first impression you might be led to believe he was perhaps some type of professional. He had clean chestnut skin with curious, charming features, jet-black hair combed into a sophisticated parting. He looked like the kind of man who might wear glasses while reading a newspaper, drink herbal tea as oppose to regular tea and maybe even have a strict vegan dietary preference. I thought it right to let him rest, his real troubles were only beginning. As I came to the end of my paper I noticed him attempting a slow painful glance down towards his right leg, one which was followed by a hot muffled groan.

'I wouldn't look down there mate, it's only going to upset you. You ain't going anywhere for a while so just try to take it easy.'

I had said more to him in the space of those few minutes than anyone else had done for the entire duration of his imprisonment. Closing his eyes he fell back into a world where he was free to go and come as he pleased. I myself had learnt the power of the imagination through weeks of solitary confinement. How it quickly becomes the prisoner's lifeboat. Everyone and everything lives in it; wife, children, parents, friends, favourite bar, most memorable holiday, perverted thought, all exist in this one surreal realm. I also learnt it can just as easily become a prisoner's worst enemy; a catalyst for rampant anxiety, a supreme tormentor, a stuttering reissue of past incidents. I learnt all this around two years ago when I assisted in the hanging of another inmate. It was a revenge attack for something that happened on the outside. I didn't ask the questions I should have asked, or the questions a person morally chained to the notions of life, death and punishment might have – a person such as myself. I'm doing life, so from how I saw it the only way I could keep that word and all its connotations from becoming totally extinct was to respond to that harsh reality with death. In retribution I found my purpose again and like most men who receive such fatal sentencing, dealing death becomes a craft, a honed skill, especially when it's to those who privately sit yearning for it.

I was already awake when he opened his eyes the following morning. We had slept next to one another throughout the night in relative harmony. His sleep was deep and lengthy. Mine intermittent. It felt strange sleeping next to another man in such helpless circumstances. When you're locked in a cell with another inmate the dynamics become almost marital. You create your own kind of dance together. On the one hand you have the man who's more passive, more feminine so to speak, then you have the dominant alpha-male, the aggressor. If those dynamics and roles aren't established from early on then there's bound to occur some kind of conflict as is customary in these high-security prisons. Men who were once powerful and feared are involuntarily stripped of their cherished ego and status, however acclaimed it may be, and forced to adopt a second-rate identity, one lesser and seemingly irrelevant. This is what inspires many of the brawls that present themselves in the prison's open spaces. The intention being to make a spectacle in the hope of gaining a more formidable reputation.

Getting up to leave I expected one of the wardens to come in and escort me to my cell but nobody came. Now I could see Robert Shah's full face as I towered above him in the way I would if I was about to place a set of flowers over the top of his coffin. Taking a long hard look it struck me again how he really didn't fit into the profiling of a prisoner, then again his kind of animal never did – it surpasses the cage and luxury of air. Becoming increasingly angered by his deplorable state I thought people like him should be locked eternally in a hole thousands of feet below ground then fed the hard skin of reptiles which had long ago died, until each individual organ becomes an incarnation of the very carrion they lived to consume. When they become thirsty and ask for water they should only be given cups of acid rain collected from the sky's most cancerous clouds.

'Who did this to me?' That was the first thing he said. His hand moving to lift away the thick tube from his mouth. A steady drip diving down into his vein. His voice sounding like a crisp packet being opened by a man with one arm.

'Nobody knows yet. I've been in here since Thursday. I only found out what happened to you through the doctor. He's an old mate. You remember anything?'

'No. I was eating, I felt something in my leg then ...'

'What they look like?'

'Who?'

'The fellas.'

'Oh, like you.'

'What's that supposed to mean?'

'White blokes. Shaven heads with tattoos.'

'I ain't trying to sound silly here mate but you've just singled out half the prison. You pissed anyone off since you been here?'

'I hardly speak to anyone.'

'Who's your cellmate?'

'Black fella. From up north. Aaron. That's all I know about him.'

'Nah, don't know him. Well just count it lucky you ain't dead. Keep your wits about you, they might be back to finish the job. Of course, that all depends on who they are and why they did it.'

I watched the panic move closer into the distressed beatings of his heart. He wasn't a tough man, anyone could see that. He wasn't a fighter. He may have been a drunk. A woman beater. A sadist. He may have dabbled in drugs, but he wasn't brave. He was a coward. A predator. I knew his kind too well. The worst breed of animal. Whatever was happening in Robert Shah's mind was enough to instil some kind of fear, the kind he would have fed his poor wife for all the years they were together. It felt right to leave him, a perspiring wreck, to taste the acid he would have once driven down her throat and into her belly. Robert Shah was feasting and overdosing on himself, a marvellous thing to see.

'Where you going?'

'Back to my cell. I've got a prison sentence to be getting on with. Can't stay tucked away in here with you, as lovely as it might be.'

'What wing you in?'

'Why, you fancy cuddling up in the evening and watching a movie?'

The corner of his lip curled up to form half a smile, but within seconds the pain in his thigh reminded him of where he was.

'Why are you here?' he said

'I had an operation,' I said.

'No, why are you here?' he repeated.

'Murder,' I said.

I tucked my white T-shirt into my trousers. At this point

most sensible inmates know to ask no further questions unless of course a rapport has been established. Robert Shah rustled around on the bed trying to get comfortable, as if he was about to watch a two hour play and wanted to make sure he had good sight-lines.

'Why?'

'You know, for a bloke who obviously ain't too popular around here you ask a lot of questions.'

'Sorry mate. I'm just anxious,' he crooned.

'Understandable.'

Zipping away my few toiletries I began walking towards the door. There was no other reason for me to stay and continue conversing with the man I knew to be Robert Shah. Robert Shah the sordid woman-beater. The ruthless murderer. The coward. In a few weeks he'll be dead. The prison having its own judicatory arrangement for people such as him. His assailants, if not found, would be guaranteed to return to finish what they unsuccessfully began. I was speaking to a marked man. A man lonely and afraid. A man who perhaps from somewhere inside that giddy fear was thinking about his dead wife and the gruesome ordeal he subjected her to. Robert Shah was a ghost. I thought then to grant him the answer to his last question, after all what harm could it have done to speak openly to him, seeing as we both knew he wouldn't live to see the closing day of the month. I sat back down on the bed.

'My missus had been having an affair for some time. I knew about it but I wasn't fit enough to sort it out. I'd become a bit of a degenerate if you know what I mean. I had a couple businesses that were doing alright, property, motors that sort of thing, but with that came a sniff habit and erm…a fondness for booze. To be honest I couldn't blame her. I was a right cunt. Working all hours, getting back at night fucked out my nut. She was happy looking after the kids, little boy and girl, twins, and carried on as if nothing out of the ordinary was happening. One evening me and an old mate arranged to meet for a few drinks, he got called to pick up his daughter from school early, she got sick or something. Anyway, I got home sooner than she must have been expecting. I opened the front door and heard screaming coming from up in the bedroom. Not like sex stuff but screaming…you know… in pain. I made it up the stairs thinking one of the kids was in trouble. I boot open the bedroom door and there they both were. The cunt was on top of her with a belt tied around her neck. Pulling it in trying to choke her. She was a fucking mess. Blood all over her face, on her stomach, everywhere. Her legs looked ripped to the point I could see her fucking bones. She was just about breathing. Fuck knows what had happened in there, all I saw when I opened the door was him bashing her over the head with like this poll thing. I couldn't make out what it was. His other hand choking her with the belt. The way her body looked on the bedroom floor, like a battered heap of shit, her legs wide apart, squirming, trying to breathe. So I…grabbed the back of his head. Smacked him once, twice, maybe a few more times. He went down. She was trying to undo the belt. I ran over to the side of the bed to get my blade.' He started to cough, first lightly then more ferociously, his chest roaring beneath the sheets. I reached over to where the water jug was, filling up his glass to bring it up to his lips. He sipped. The cough eased. A clear lace of water streamed from out his left eye, down the side of his head and over his ear. I waited with the water-jug in my hand for his breathing to recalibrate itself.

'Cheers mate.' Lumps of phlegm drumming against his vocal chords.

'What you do to him?' he asked with slight apprehension.

Abruptly I put the water-jug back on the unit. 'Hacked half his fucking head off. I would have finished if she hadn't tried to stop me. I don't know how far I got. He was wailing like a pig, blood squirting everywhere. I couldn't kill him enough. She jumped on my back. Punching, scratching saying I'd killed him. I threw her off. She whacked her head on the edge of the bed's frame. Steel. Died just like that. They gave me a life sentence for him, manslaughter for her. Either way, I ain't going anywhere for a while … I loved her, I really fucking did. She shouldn't have died like that, she shouldn't have died like that, and I shouldn't have been the fuck up I was.'

If he was able to reach out maybe he would have put an arm on my shoulder or say he understood but he didn't, instead Robert Shah lay steadily breathing with his mouth agape. Despite his nebulous gaze something inside of me suspected I was retelling a drama he had at some point already seen or maybe even experienced himself. Those who in their lives have been exposed to certain unimaginable afflictions, to the point where they become numb and impervious to any further distresses, carry within them an oddity which always manages to make itself apparent when things of this nature are brought up. For Robert Shah there was nothing upsetting about my crime or the savagery behind my intent. He internalised my life's history with acceptance, like a solid aspirin being dropped into a glass of cold water, allowing it to dissolve into a clear amorphous calm.

I made another attempt to leave and let him brood on the remaining few days he had left as Robert Shah. Turning my back I felt a strange sense of violation come over me. Something conniving and intrusive had just happened with the same invisible magic a pick-pocket might deploy on the city's crowds. Robert Shah had managed to subtly extract the most harrowing story of my life without reciprocating anything in return; no sympathetic token, not even a mere reconciliation. No understanding, no infuriation. He heard my story yet I still knew nothing of his. Only his name and the fickle rumours which circulated the prison on his arrival.

'Why are you here?' I asked.

'I was stabbed,' he replied.

'No, why are you here?' I asked again.

'Murder,' he said.

Robert Shah, with little reluctance, went on to recount the many incidences that made up the bulk of his wasted life. The events presented me with enough evidence to know him before he killed his wife. Before he was hated on and in turn was taught to hate viciously back. A progeny of violence and fear, he spoke for nearly thirty-five minutes about what he would come to call his life. His voice finding strength and pace, regaining that smooth able musicality which for so long had been stagnant and undisturbed. I remained on the edge of the bed listening to the wickedness and horrors of his childhood; the rape and irregular torture inflicted by his older cousin, the lack of resistance, the fight for authority, the need for power and dominance between his parents and his uncles. How all this was borne in silence. I listened in the same adiaphorous way he had done. At the closing sentence the strength in his voice began to suffer the punishment of frailty for its rebellion. Even monsters at some point had to have loved something outside of the violence they so frequently invented, so finally I asked what his job was.

'I am,' he corrected himself, ' I was, a gardener. Had my own little business. A few blokes working for me, about six all together. Left school, needed a job, my neighbour needed help, said I could work with him for a bit. Raking leaves, weeding, simple shit. Two years I was there, taught me to do it all.' He stopped, his mouth dry, his words sticking to his gums. Extending a hand he slowly reached for the glass of water beside him, grimacing from the pain. His extension unable to clasp the half filled glass so I got up, putting the water into his hands again, trying to steady the tremor as he took down small infant sips, nodding to signal he'd had enough.

'Everyone has one recurring thought in here don't they?'

'One? I don't think anyone's that lucky mate,' I said.

'Maybe I am. When I was a kid I remember always hiding in the back of my old mum's garden, away from all the fights and her dirty boyfriends. It felt safe there.

All them colours. You know how kids do stupid shit? I used to think each flower was like a mate, a girlfriend or something. I used to cry a lot in those days, especially in the back of the garden. Summers were the worst. All the flowers would start to spring up. I would tell myself all the fucking tears I cried were causing these flowers to pop up from the ground. I tried to make myself stop, but I couldn't. Like tears were these mad little seeds that would burst into things the moment they hit the ground. It's weird. Over time I learnt to be delicate with flowers. I had patience but my missus…she was the most dangerous flower of them all. The only one I couldn't rip out and tear up when I wanted. I was reckless sometimes, pulling out and stomping on everything I could, the more beautiful something looked the more it drove me mad. I wanted it dead. The boys would ask what the matter was but I'd say nothing. I'd be ripping out what I wanted when I wanted. But mate…my missus, she was fucking wild and I hated her for it. The way she could take herself away like that. Disappear completely. In her mind. Always writing shit down. Always looking fucking peaceful. I'd come home and she'd be staring out the window, at the parked cars, the people in street, writing, writing, writing, all the time, never asking how my day was, never saying she missed me or she loved me. I never got that. That's when I'd lose it, you know. Bit by bit, it started off with a little slap then I just wanted to get heavier. You think one more hit, one more and I won't hate her anymore, but I just couldn't hurt her enough. For all the time I've been banged up in here that's all I can think about. Maybe all I ever wanted was to sit on her side of the garden, under her sun, but she just wouldn't show me how to get there.'

We'd both said enough. The warden who was keeping guard outside came in to escort me to my cell. Within days news regarding the prison stabbing started to spread, as did more details surrounding the atrocities of Robert Shah's violence. Having learnt where he hid his last bit of luck, the three inmates who attempted to take his life returned not long after he was acquitted from the infirmary. Robert Shah was found hanging in his cell by the guards at around 7.35am. A putrid pool of faeces and urine shimmering beneath his feet with a face beaten raw and bloody. The hospital bandage around his stab wound still absorbing those daubs of pointless blood. Righteously the men nailed a cutout of St George's Cross into his chest, the same side where his heart would have thumped its final beat. I told them to put a fresh yellow daffodil in his trouser pocket once they were done, for his wife.

Cowboy

There were nights when her mother would stand by her bedroom door just to watch her. She was of course supposed to be asleep, but when a mother has to work late it grants the child an opportunity to take advantage of the big night and its inviting solitude.

We could see her dolls meticulously aligned in the corner of her room opposite the window where the curtains were always kept widely drawn. Blonde dolls, more female than male with pinkish skin and coarse hair placed up by the skirting. Each one's frame resembling the other with its factory set of small rounded breasts, protruding bottom and flat beach-like stomach. All favourably ranked in order of popularity and beauty, while being made to purposefully appear as if they were forever holding hands. As the line fell into the shadows, we could see the dolls which bore the forsaken marks, scars and blemishes of those old and least preferred, buried in the room's sunless corner where they remained forgotten by everyone except time.

With the plastic of their skin and bones she had created the perfect panoply of a family life she knew must exist, however this wasn't what worried her mother. Rather it was the sight of seeing her young daughter play tirelessly with one particular plastic figure. He, like the others, had pinkish skin, cinematic blue eyes, blond hair, and a broad hexagonal chest with thick muscular legs. He wore a white and blue cowboy hat with a gun lodged brazenly in the holster around his waist. His grin dictating to the rest of his facial features what they should always be doing. Her mother tried hard to remember who brought the toy for her. Maybe her father had, one of the few gifts he ever surprised her with. On this particular night she interrupted the young girl's play by what we assume was her asking why she wasn't in bed, and why she was up so late playing with her dolls and cowboy. Here, one might expect a young daughter to grow mildly effervescent at hearing the voice of a mother she hadn't seen all day. Not her. Instead she aloofly reeled the figure into her pyjama pocket, remarking with the candour of the young, that she really wished she could be a cowboy.

As the years developed we know her mother was forced to change jobs several times, although no substantial reason was ever given as to why, which could have helped to appease the growing tensions between them. She kept few friends, her repose finding itself in the introverted hours she would spend drawing alone. Most of her illustrations consisted of white unicorns, bright hot-air balloons and tropical fish. Things indigenous to one's imagination, the massless air or tepid oceanic shallows.

Her best friend's name was Holly. We know that from the summer days they spent skipping and playing in the front garden until being called in for tea. Their mothers met one year at a school committee meeting where they were brought into a conversation about property development and the benefits of gentrification. Her mother liked Holly. That was known. She seemed bright and intelligent. Sociable and duly polite. The perfect balance for someone like her daughter, who most of the time appeared to posses all the sad qualities of a person who was, by and large, socially inept.

Within the tombs of silence and seclusion there is a certain kind of clarity. From quietude's expansive tunnels the ear and soul's most poignant faculties rouse those enchanting senses, the ones unattainable to the mass of people who prefer the fanfare and clutter of everyday living. In her early teens she gradually adopted a capacity for hermeticism. She noticed how her mother would start arriving home later and later from work. How she skipped meals, settling instead for a bottle of red wine and a flickering television screen that spoke often but said nothing. On the few occasions the young girl wasn't home, we assume she was staying over at Holly's house. It would be here where she probably noticed a similar turn of events to the ones she encountered at home. The only difference being Holly's mother could fall promisingly into the comfort of the arms that wrapped themselves around her, delicately kissing the crown of her head. A sight she had only partially seen in the plastic world of her dolls and their innocuous sensibilities.

This was continuous throughout the next few years that she lived at home with her mother. Then, just like that, she grew into the shape of a young woman, one whose exact age remained frustratingly unknown. Her childhood toys turned dead and grave-less, scattered somewhere in the buried lengths of her mother's attic. From what we know by this time she had kissed one boy, as well as having learnt to fix bicycles, repair punctures, install brakes and wear her hair in different ways. The kiss itself happened out on the street around five years ago and only a few yards away from her mother's front door.

It was summer, so understandably everything was looking to be loved. The young boy had complimented her by saying she had nice lips and how the smell of her hair reminded him of his sister. Coquettishly she returned the compliment remarking how he had nice coloured eyes, and how he reminded her of a toy cowboy she once had when she was a girl. That's when he leant forward to kiss her. Both of them feeling like new stars discovering the immortality of the universe. His hands starting their precarious descent down into the parts of her female body he had only been allowed to visit during hot masturbatory nights, ones where his older brother was either out or asleep. With a steely grip she motioned his hand away, as if placing something that wasn't ever needed back on the shop shelf. Firmly, she said something along the lines of you might look like a cowboy but that doesn't mean you should act like one.

It wasn't long before the young cowboy disappeared for good. His parents moving to another part of the city, taking with them her first kiss and the eager hands she so surely denied. After that awkward encounter the young girl said to herself that boys weren't important. She thought of her mother and the way she dealt with loneliness and longing. She thought of her father and his perpetual absence, then finally she concluded there were perhaps other things teenage girls could concern themselves with. However, to maintain such a staunch, iconoclastic philosophy was difficult, especially when boys were always the main subject of conversation among her small group of friends. Growing tired of such senseless chit-chat she chose instead to draw and paint, using an abstraction of colours capable of reflecting her various moods. An aberrant, mystified solace was discovered, gradually nurtured by the whirling currents of art and hue. Laying on her front each night she could effortlessly summon whatever was envisioned within using the body of just one simple colour, just one swaying stroke. Soon this was to become her greatest past time.

One night she walked into the living room to speak with her mother. Instantly she was struck by the way the candle's flame could make her mother's wine glass materialise into something supremely rich. A shimmering pool of maroon suspended sombrely over the candle's balmy gold. She stood watching. On the sideboard there lay one of her many notepads, unlined, with a black biro attached to it. She drew what she saw, letting the minutes amble past her until the flame eventually flickered and died, leaving the bottle to loom in its transparent emptiness. The glass now looked repellently stained, tainted with the bodiless blood of her mother's French wine. Who would now want to sketch such a poor aesthetic? The young girl stood inanimately, steady in the gallows of her own private sorrow, her etched illustration begging for more life, begging to be completed. She observed sadly the way her mother's vinous sleep almost crushed her distinguished beauty, the pride of her shoulders, the articulacy of her speech. Her suit jacket still on and crumpled. Her mouth agape with teeth the colour of a cremated sky. Her breath godless and rancid. Then came the clawing urge to ask her why? Why was she doing this to herself? Why wasn't she in bed? Why was she up this late? Why was she letting the thing within destroy her so easily? Habitually she looked around the room for the plastic figure of a toy cowboy but there was nothing, only bits of chic furniture that nobody would ever come to admire. She stubbed out the thoughts on the ashtray of her fate, the same one where so much quantifiable ash had accumulated to linger and putrefy. Glancing down she ran her eyes over the sketch she made. It looked rough and inaccurate. She hated it. Turning off the television, then closing the living-room door, she made her way to bed, leaving her mother on the sofa, drunk and dreamless.

After some months the mother attacked her daughter. She broke her nose with one barbarous jab. Like most devastating events, it was the kind of thing that happened within seconds but had been ominously manifesting for months, or perhaps even years. Her mother was by now almost constantly intoxicated and morbidly lonely. From what's known, it's believed the first signs of trouble began to manifest when the young girl brought up the subject of a boy she was dating. One evening, while eating dinner, the two spoke affably about the day's events when in mid-conversation the name Alex was voiced by the young daughter. This was the first time her mother had heard her daughter say a man's name at the dinner table. Alex. With an unripe lemon in her throat she asked who this boy was and how they had met. The young daughter casually responded saying they'd known each other since college, that he was a good friend of Holly's boyfriend and they were now officially a couple.

News of the boyfriend was relayed roughly a week before the assault, meaning her mother would have had sufficient time to dangerously ruminate on the impending reality which was propelling her daughter closer towards finding her one true love – a love she herself was in desperate need of. Within the next few days there were numerous bouts of unresolved conflict between the two. Everything grew discernibly tense. Each feud found its motive in the most trivial of incidences. The mother developing a twisted compulsion to undermine her daughter's life-long ambition. Dreadful things were expressed, screamed and repeated. She would scorn her daughter for being who she was, or worse still, for who she wanted to become. She referred to her, in the heat and slur of words poisoned by wine and misery, as some mediocre artist plagued by indolence, branding her a spoilt rich-girl, one who had only been afforded the luxury of her apparent artsy aspiration through the diligence and privilege provided by her own single-handed success. Collectively her words ripped at the young girl's darkened eyes, until the warring sky containing all her sorrows was at last ruptured, opening the way for a successive rush of salt-water that drowned everything she desperately fought to conceal.

The assault itself occurred on a Wednesday night at around 10.30pm. Earlier that evening her daughter announced she would soon be leaving home. She said Alex and her were in the process of making plans to move in together. Another heated dispute followed, one that was to segue into the daughter raising the very sensitive and volatile issue of her mother's uncontrollable drinking. She was aware that in the course of the past month her mother had already called in sick five times, a truism which helped strengthen her belief that her alcoholism had now become frighteningly insuppressible. Haughtily her mother stated those days were in fact not sick days but holiday-leave, and the time taken off was time officially owed to her. Sharp gambits were rapidly exchanged cutting through the neighbourhood's stillness. Harsh and vulgar words such as Bitch, Liar, Disgusted, Whore and Shame were all cast upon the other indiscriminately, until finally the daughter passively capitulated, allowing the mother to reclaim her much needed dominance.

Peevishly, with wine wading through her system, the mother lit her final cigarette, flinging the empty packet across the glass coffee table, inhaling deep, absorbing drags from the stick's orange-speckled butt. The bickering escalated until the mother's punch launched itself straight into the daughter's enraged face. A shambolic hullabaloo epitomising the disastrous and exasperating tie a family such as theirs had come to engender. The last thing the daughter heard was the boorish tonality her mother raged in before shrilling the phrase Little Bitch, accompanied by an enervated, inexact strike of her right arm. The daughter spilling back into the neat parade of kitchen chairs, her body no longer hers, covered her face while wailing down into the clean terracotta tiles. Realising what she'd done her mother came floundering over. Crying. Blubbering stifled sounds. Blood on both their white tops. Deep red splurges coated the pine furniture making it quite clear their relationship had now reached its anticipated end. The mother may not have intended to break the daughter's nose, or kill whatever remained of their timorous bond, after-all, that part may have been accidental – alcohol having played such a pivotal role in the turn of these tragic events. Yet what assumably took the mother over the proverbial edge wasn't the boyfriend, or even the comments regarding her drinking, it was in fact the stark announcement that her daughter would soon be moving out of home to start a new life with the man who she apparently loved. The man whose name was first aired at the kitchen table a few days prior to the incident. The man whose name we know to be Alex.

All this change undoubtedly proved to be way too much for her mother. Unbeknown to her enamoured daughter who was up until then still addled by the nature of such exciting love, were the undisclosed feelings her mother had painfully amassed over the course of those few days – even before any mention came of her daughter and the boyfriend moving out. Feelings that most likely emerged on the evening she found out her daughter was now lost in the undertow of insensible love. A silent truth which deprived her of a whole night's sleep, involuntarily spending those nocturnal hours wide awake, fatefully steeped in expensive wine, envisioning the two of them both laying in a bedroom naked, her painting as he did whatever it was he did. He wasn't important. He didn't matter. It was his arms that troubled her. His touch. His affection. The amorous ways he would be kissing her before they began making love. His face in the morning, waking up next to hers so as to make love all over again, but obviously she couldn't let the daughter know the way her jealousy styled itself.

It looked like the daughter's nose was either broken or fractured, her eyes heavily blackened and her tears running superfluously down her face. Her mother hurtling around the kitchen looking for a tea towel to stop the bleeding while at the same time trying to remind the daughter to keep her head tilted back. To keep looking up at the ceiling. She didn't want to call an ambulance; the thought of those lacerating neon strobes infiltrating the midnight hour causing meddlesome neighbours to peep through their curtains, or stand apprehensively in their doorways in only dressing gowns and slippers.

At this point, between the bombardment of apologies and words intended to offer some kind of comfort, her mother claimed the reason she had lashed out wasn't because her only daughter would be moving out, or for the fact she was now in love with this boy named Alex, but because she knew, in her heart of hearts, that they would want to move into the flat together. The flat she purchased for her daughter all those years ago with the intention of having her move into the property once she was a bit more mature, with a burgeoning career, both stable and purposeful. She was working in a small art shop selling paints, canvasses and random artwork created by a handful of relatively unknown local artists. Her mother constantly reminding her how the job offered very few prospects, that she couldn't do it forever and she would need to take some time out to think about what it was she really wanted to do, but more importantly that this wasn't where she hoped for her to be at this stage in her life.

Now, what really irked the mother was whenher daughter had previously disclosed her plans to move she used very specific words such as Independence, Space and Peace of Mind followed by Boyfriend, Love, Security, Dreams and Art. In her mother's mind Alex was merely filling a carnal purpose, a plastic figure to play with in times of boredom when there was nothing else to occupy the night. We know that's how she regarded most men; as mindless and primitive entities who should only be beckoned in those more concupiscent hours, yet in her daughter's mind Alex was so much more. He wasn't just a man, he was someone replenishing a void comprised of both ontological and intimate necessity. He would protect her, sleep beside her, hold her, adore her in the intricate ways only he could. She would be his and he would be hers.

With the cloth still pressed up against her nose she sourly mentioned Holly had already moved into an East

London flat with her boyfriend and that their young union had fortified itself. They spent evenings drinking and dining in local restaurants, enjoying the fine range of foreign cuisine with other young popinjays. She reiterated how rent wouldn't be an issue but if her mother really did disapprove of the move then they were happy to find another place to live. Her mother however was more than aware this would be impossible as her daughter's wage packet was mortifyingly minimal and from the little she'd been told about Alex, his job was equally poor.

Bringing the cloth away from her nose she insisted they'd done all the maths and were capable of matching the rate the current tenants were already paying. Her mother went back over to pour the last helping of wine into her glass, looking at her daughter with the white tablecloth blotted with blood on her lap. The bleeding had subsided and this, to both their relief, informed them that the nose wasn't in fact broken. Her mother placed a finger under her daughter's chin, tilting back her head slightly to inspect more closely the damage. Taking the cloth from her lap and walking over to the laundry she asked what he did for work. Touching with gentle pinches the ridge of her nose she said he was currently delivering pizzas but he was planning to start work for his uncle's construction company in the next few weeks, emphasising he too had big dreams, ones he had carefully grasped from the loose apparitions of his boyhood.

The two didn't speak properly for some time after the incident but eventually the mother came to appreciate her daughter's point of view, accepting that her little girl was indeed growing up and that her own latent misery had rooted itself in a part of her which had little to do with her daughter's actual affairs. She understood during the course of those following weeks how people can develop a capacity to lie to the world but never to themselves. From what's known she never did hit her mother back nor did the mother hit her daughter again, even though there were still some disputes and grievances, right up until the Tuesday when Alex drove round in a small black Ford to help move his girlfriend's belongings into their new flat.

Things haven't seemed this amicable for months. Her mother stands endearingly by the front door in a thick white dressing gown, puffing unsteadily on a slim cigarette while reeling off a checklist of things her daughter needs to do once she gets into the flat. Deliberately she avoids having to exchange words with the man who in a few moments will have inadvertently purloined her only daughter. He doesn't appear to mind as he walks in and out of the house carrying a new box each time, his face burdened with its own obtrusive worry. One of the great advantages of youth is how it can masterfully conceal despair in a singular beauty, one exclusive to such undeveloped age, a despair that only the old and infirm can recognise after having lived through its regrettably short artifice. Marked boxes are being piled into the car. Then comes the closing act. At the door the mother and daughter embrace for a long period of time. Holding each other. Needing each other. Until everything is made to feel as if it's been restored; her daughter clinging on to her body as she did those twenty-one years ago when her mother laboured and screamed through excruciating pains just to hand this little life over to the world. Alex sits in the car waiting patiently, the boxes layered with masking tape all loaded unevenly in the boot and the back seat. Her mother asks if she has everything she needs; her daughter sends back an affectionate nod, keeping a hand on her mother's thin arm for reassurance, asking her not to worry. She will be in touch in a few days. After they'd managed to settle in and unpack some bits.

The car indicates to pull out onto the street, the squashed plastic figure of a cowboy with a white and blue hat, pinkish skin, cinematic blue eyes, blond hair and a broad hexagonal chest pokes out from the top of one of the boxes. It looks to be the same as it was, even after all this time. Off he goes making the final journey, his ageless and exact face pressed up against the car's back window. Within seconds she was gone, as was he – lost to the great gamble of life and love.

With that I stepped away from the window handing the room back to its soft and retracted light. Settling into my armchair I remembered today was Tuesday and my afternoon tea would soon be arriving. Next to the remote control was a letter from my daughter. All it said was Dad, please will you call us. The postage stamp on the envelope was marked U.S.A. There were two separate telephone numbers on the bottom of the letter – one longer than the other. Putting my spectacles on I studied both for some time. Then I folded it once, twice, three times, until it became no smaller than a pill, burying it inside my glasses case just beneath the cleaning cloth. Looking around the room I remembered again today was Tuesday and my afternoon tea would soon be arriving. I glanced down at my watch, the one she bought me just after my retirement. I readjusted the strap. It had just gone 1.30pm. Picking up the remote control I flicked through the channels – One, Two, Three, Four. It's old. I turned it off. It still couldn't pick up a clear picture. Food should be here soon I thought. Better keep an eye out.

Belongings

The last voice you heard was hers. She gave you sufficient warning. To take all your belongings with you when you leave. To leave behind nothing capable of reminding her that you were once a part of this home. That you existed here together. That she was once yours and you were once hers. You have reached the moment when everything you tried to build together starts its long, piteous crumble. It's the end, and like the previous endings you've suffered you find yourself once again reeling back to the very beginning; maybe in an attempt to identify a reason, or maybe because those embryonic months, where everything was formed from the votive cloth of rainbows, held within them the soothing balm to your underlying heartache.

You have a long way to go, that's what you tell yourself as the oscillating progression provokes your thoughts. You shift back to the time you came into each other's worlds, a time when neither of you believed in endings. When you drove away from her mother's house in your modest car, her wiping away the tears along with the bad memories, while you held her hand whispering words of assurance laced in legitimate promises. As is common with new lovers, both pure in purpose, you wanted to become each other, to beam a steady light through the bleak reality of each other's tunnels, bend with each other's smoke, let each other's name hold the vows your mouths so readily declared. In time you grew to understand the language of her nature. The way she stretched her limbs out towards the sky in the early mornings before work. How she rubbed loose the bits of gathered sleep from the puffy pockets of her eyes. She would be the first and last thing you'd see. Even before you had set sight on the day's texture outside, before you'd even checked the time, you were already looking straight into the eyelashes of her great sun.

You found joy in those tepid irises of hers, the kind that left you looking at your own happiness blind. How wonderful it was. Her smile. Your smile. How beautiful it was to love the same person over and over again. To make plans of devoting an entire lifetime to preserving and recreating that love. One which lives in tribute to the very first love that met you both in those younger years. To feel the strain of life become lessened by those soft and succinct expressions of a heart that can only beat so long as yours is alive to beat with it. Words that can only be, so long as your ears are around to receive them. How wonderfully it all presented itself; to rest in love, to know with all your days you were both safe, keeping a part of yourselves open for the other to fall into and find healing once again. How love patterns itself so flawlessly.

Before she had stepped into her morning shower you already knew the tune she would sing. And you would sing along too, just because she was, but you would do so discreetly, as if bashfully sharing an unofficial prayer with the perfect temple of your happy heart. Familiar, like already knowing the colours of the clothes she would wear. Bright colours. Celebratory. Because today would be spent in love. Doubled and proud. Rejoicing in a safe and limitless love, one that carefully guided you to the acme of all ardency, then allowed you to bellow forever-songs from the rich mountain of your heart.

Everything would be learnt in time. Like the map of a repeated journey you would observe things about her with an almost surgical eye. The way her scent would change from day to day depending on her mood. How the colours she'd wear would deepen or intensify depending on the quality of her feelings. Now you sit in the carriage holding onto your few belongings, not the ones in your hand but the ones inside yourself as the reality transports you further away from her. You travel deeper into the distance as it begins to make you its own. You think about the first time you kissed her and you deny your eyes the cool rivers they so despairingly want to free. The first kiss was so strange, so awkward and exultant. Her lips warm and accurate; a kiss loaded with so much loneliness, so much searching and deprivation.

Now, your throbbing mind amidst all its toil and conflict searches for a reason to hate her, even though you're unable to because your heart won't permit it. It still belongs to her, sleeping somewhere in her arms until she'll inadvertently roll over to crush it. You kick the seat with your heel startling the lady next to you who happens to be holding a carrier bag with a new sketchpad and some paints inside. You make your assumption. Apologising with the embarrassment stuck to your tone. She smiles. It keeps moving. Your mind. The memories. Stop at the park. The park. The bucolic tranquility where couples and families flock when needing to reacquaint themselves with things made by the hand of the sky rather than by the machine. Where they unleash the tender spirit of love and lounge in its great rapture. Everything is permitted to be unusual and mad. No longer mythopoeic. No longer restrained.

You're at the still lake with the half-dozen swans. You're remembering how she loved to paint them in her summer sketchbook while you lazed on the grass beside her, dipping low the white and blue cowboy hat she bought you for your twenty-fourth birthday, resting its rim coolly just above your eyes. She wanted to be an artist so much, painting and drawing profusely as you lay beside her under the warmth of the sun, sipping a cold bottle of beer, feeling the earth against your skin, watching as her paintbrush danced and leaked around the anaemic walls of the pad. How she would carefully braid together the small range of colours she had, capturing the regal grace of those noble swans. Bright. Celebratory. How she would say that in her past life she must have been a swan. Or a cowboy. You can't recall much more than that but you do remember the comment you made about her neck, how it was elongated and swan-like. She leaned in to kiss you, taking off your hat dumping it childishly on her head. She told you then how you'd saved her, but you couldn't quite grasp what she'd meant. That was the year you finally understood summer.

You exhale. It's becoming increasingly difficult to breathe. Thoughts building up to harass your lungs. You hear her calling your name. In your head. It's faint like syllables being submersed in water. In oceans. A man boards. He's carrying shopping. You notice a bottle of red wine, six free-range eggs with various dips. He wears brogues. His aftershave newly applied. His skin smooth. His hair neat. Someone is waiting for him somewhere.

You spent all day preparing the meal. It was February 14th. Valentine's day. Summer had long gone. You were out of work, again. You thought it would be nice to have her come home to a surprise. It excited you to envision her excited. Flowers. Bright with life. Wine. Red for love and passion and blood. Her favourite cuisine. Jazz music swaying from your old record player. Coltrane. Her favourite. The plan: she walks in from work, closes the door, puts her bag down then makes her way over to the living room. There she would be halted by sheer astonishment. Her face would ignite, her perfect teeth revealing themselves. Then with a shy incredulity she would express a sentiment overflowing with love and appreciation, noticing how you had meticulously arranged the room to be almost shrine-like. The pictures of you both polished on the shelf. The aroma of food wafting in from the kitchen. The mellifluous sound of music. The wine. Candles. Low-lighting. How handsome you will look – all for her.

You cooked all day. Thai chicken curry. Her favourite. You found the recipe online. You burnt yourself twice. Cut yourself once. She would be home in half an hour. You hurry. Hoover. Dust again. The parts you missed. Fold the clothes. The bright ones. Put them away. Wash the dishes. Move as if you didn't live there and everything she was about to see happened within the context of some unexplainable miracle. Rearrange the fridge magnets to spell I Love You Babe. Her keys jangle in the door. She opens and sees you standing there, smiling your most sincere smile. You're wearing a newly pressed shirt, black trousers and polished brogues. You've shaved for once and put on cologne. The only one on your shelf, the one she bought you, her favourite. Your books stacked away neatly. Coltrane is playing low. Track three. Her favourite. She smiles an uncomfortable smile. Forced. The wrong kind of smile. It catches you off guard. She's tired, you can see that. She doesn't say anything. Her bags look as if they're carrying her. She doesn't kiss your lips. She doesn't comment on the smell of the food or the music playing low. She doesn't become emphatic over the bottle of wine or your polished brogues. She can't smell your cologne. She walks slowly into the bedroom. The same you would whisper her morning shower songs in. She closes the door leaving you on the outside with John Coltrane playing perfectly oblivious.

It's getting busier. Must be rush hour. Nobody wants to acknowledge the other person. The only words exchanged are excuse me. Can you move down a bit please. Sorry. People are bunched in together doing their best to avoid eye contact. Re-reading the same adverts. Adverts that say nothing. You bring your belongings in, closer towards you. More pile in. A lady wearing a suit as grey as her hair opens the evening paper. She hovers above you. The headline reads Storm Warning. Your vest starts to stick to your skin. You're perspiring. You start to read the article in the hope it'll take your mind off things but it's difficult, too much jostling around. You pick out what you can: Gales of up to 80mph winds. Heavy rains. Torrential. Danger. Strong storms. Met Office. Three people dead. Drowning dog.

Drowning dog.

Money was tight. You were still out of work. She was supporting you, covering the rent with her wages from the art shop. You knew that. Every weekend she would try and explain to her mother that things were getting better. Every weekend she would cry after hanging up the phone. You had lost two jobs. Nobody wanted to employ you. You had no experience in anything substantial. She bought the food. You cleaned the house. Washed dishes, even the clean ones. Ironed clothes. Read books. Wrote. That weekend the rains came down heavy. She was feeling low. Said she wanted to stay in bed. You hated seeing her like that. Crushed. Pale. Unwashed. You told her a joke to try and lift the mood. It started with do you remember the time when and ended with you laughing alone. You brought her over a cup of tea but by the close of the hour it was cold.

The rain was everywhere. Noisy rain, continuous and confident. You suggested a trip to the pet shop. She loved the pet shop, always full of innocent laniferous creatures, all excitable and wanting love, wanting a home, a place to belong. She opened her eyes and made her way into the shower. She washed in silence, water all around. At the pet shop she hunkered down by a puppy's cage. A Pomeranian. Her fingers affectionately stroking its wet nose whispering into its bewildered harmlessness until she decided she wanted it. You rubbed her back saying you'd buy it for her. Her face immediately reborn vaulting upwards. She kissed your cheeks. Not your lips, just your cheeks. But then you said you couldn't buy it today, you would come back next month. The issue with money and work.

The arms which she placed around your neck started undoing themselves, like a choreographed routine and metaphor which writers will try to portray in stories using the medium of language in an attempt to symbolise the dissolving effects of love. Her kiss retracting. Her lips drying. You had no money. What were you thinking? Maybe you felt guilty? Maybe you wanted to show how much her happiness meant to you? Or how you were willing to put it above yours seeing as you've never wanted pets. You even claimed once how they require a love you're unable to provide. On the bus home neither of you spoke. She leered through the window outlining broken-hearted shapes in the condensation with her finger. The bus approached the stop and you both got off. Walking, she took your hand saying she was actually glad you didn't buy the pup. She was glad you were broke and she was supporting you. You said nothing. Your stomach was a heaving concoction of anger and shame. She stated if you had bought her the dog she would have drowned it within a week, because no creature had the right to live such an easy life.

Stop. Stationed for nearly five minutes. Signal failure further down the line. Your mind can hate her a bit more now but your heart overrides it, you try to focus on something else but can't. You rely on terrible memories like this in times of hurting. You know why bad things happen in relationships? So later on you're able to reflect and understand why that relationship was never worth keeping. To help restore a sense of equanimity amidst all the chaos. It makes sense now doesn't it?

Looking down at your rucksack you pore over its contents. Two pairs of underwear, a toothbrush, a deodorant can, two pairs of socks, two second-hand shirts, a pair of jeans and your shoes. Nothing worth keeping. What about your books? You'll have to go back for them. You forgot the cowboy hat too. She'll probably throw it out. You decide that when you get off you too will throw away everything inside the bag. You don't need belongings, who does? That's what you say to yourself. They're ruinous and what's more they weigh good people down.

You envision yourself tipping the bag into the first dustbin you find, but then, as if your own private tormentor had woken, you think of the other belongings you're holding, the ones you can't just dump into the first dustbin you pass. This upsets you. Again you try place your mind elsewhere. Somewhere free from her smell, her fingers and the way she would tuck her leg inside yours when she slept. Shake it off. There's more to life than love.

You know this. You think of doing things alone. Eating. Walking. Watching television. Going to the cinema. She's never experienced proper loneliness. You can tell by the way she treats your heart. The lonely can never be that reckless. There's peace of mind out there somewhere you tell yourself. A beach. A sunset. The waves. Infinity. You feel your blood begin to suffuse easing the tension around your shoulders. You release the lock of your jaw. Emotions ebb back. New vistas. You even go so far as to nod your head in a strange nirvanic accord, one you've just made with yourself. You feel good despite the aforementioned circumstances, despite your loss, your lack of belongings and your laden heart. You think more about the beach until it delivers you into the perfect repose, but then like a vacation which reaches fruition too soon, her name manages to muscle its way into the chimera, as if she had just skimmed a stone on the serenity of your sterling shores.

Skimming stones. It was something you always said you could do, having learnt the technique from your father when you were a boy. Make sure you find one that's not just flat but light too. It's a lot trickier than people think. You spoke like a true expert. Like a person who had won awards for stone skimming. You reiterated your point that the best stones held the capacity to travel far into the sea's distance. Riding its back. Understanding its temperament. You spoke with fervour as if the little stones defined you, as if you made them with your bare hands and she stood listening with all the adoration she held, all the elation swimming madly in the endless joys of her young face.

Half way through your lecture on stone skimming she interjected to declare her love for you. She stressed while being gripped by the throes of passion that you were indeed weird and eccentric, but never had she loved anyone quite as much as she loved you. In your hand you held tight the perfect stone, one you pilfered from the body of the mighty shore, but you were in love and lovers have no business holding onto such things. You dropped it there at your feet, as if it was wrong and you were replacing it with something right. You kissed her until the waves came to soak both your shoes. But wait, what about the beach? The rapture and serenity? The image had now lost its appeal. It just killed itself. Its lifeboat lay punctured. Its crew capsized. Movement again. You were heading further into deeper tunnels. Further into darkness and you had nobody's light now but your own.

Can you stop pushing me. Let go. Relax. Let go. I will but you need to stop pushing me. Fucking let me go. You can't make it out. What's happening. People are looking over to the right by the door. There's a dispute between a man and a woman. You're not thinking about her anymore. But you are. You just did. Shut up. Distraction. Look, I was only trying to get past you. Really, by putting your hand on my arse? I've got no room to move, it was an accident. Your elbow is in my back. It's not, look. Stop shoving. It's these two behind me. Just let go. How when I've got nowhere else to move. Let go. But if you let go she will throw boiling water over you again. She will take each and every one of your books and rip them to pieces. Snap your records in half. She will do these things with all the violence in her heart. So what do you do? You squeeze her wrist to stop the vandalism but she brings a knee up to find the softest part of your stomach. She lands a punch to the back of your head. Followed by another one. You hear it ring through your skull. Another one to the ribs. They all connect. You're hurt. You try to grab the other wrist but it's too difficult. She's fast. Why don't you just hit her back? This isn't the first time she's behaved like this. You hurl your body into her. You think of the scar on your right ear ramming her into the drying clothes that still smell of summer. You're shouting. She's screaming. Hit her. Defend yourself. But you don't. She calls you a cunt. Once. Twice. Cunt. Cunt. Cunt. Spits in your face. Malodorous. Venomous spit. You get up. Insane. Only animals spit you yell. You pound your head against the wall with all the ferociousness of a savage. By the third blow you're on the floor. Bleeding. Your head's cut. Blood. She's above you. Shaking you. Hysterical. You can hear but can't speak. The blood leaves your head. Everything feels warm. Like someone's just placed a hot flannel over your forehead. It trickles down into your eyes, streams over your face to find your open mouth. You drink. Drown and gurgle. Replenishing the life that escapes you. You want to be dead. You need to be dead. Why can't you be dead? She cries until you regain consciousness. You're together at the hospital, both concerned, both holding each other's hand. You say you're a rugby player. You use the term occupational hazard then joke casually about masculinity. The stitches work their way into your scalp as she rubs your back in the same way you rubbed hers at the pet shop. For the next two weeks you're struck by a series of irregular headaches, but for some reason hanging up the clothes to dry hurts more than anything else.

The lady gets off at the next stop. Always. First. The lady leaves. Things on the carriage settle down. Two months after that fight she leaves. The last one. You wonder if this is how things resolve themselves. How couples patch things up. You don't hear from her for a while. She avoids your calls and texts. She's with friends apparently. Hollie and co. The universal refuge for the assailed and lost. You check online. Profile page. Looking for activity. New friends? Keep scrolling. You read books. Play records alone. Drink tea. Look for work. You notice the plants more. You remember conversations you had about gardens. You water them each day and marvel at the magnificence of their colours. You watch nature documentaries for more colours. Bright. Celebratory. She comes home after a month of absence. You've lost weight and your beard's grown thick. She makes no comment. She says bluntly she wants to talk. You sit in the front room on opposite sides of the sofa. After a tentative silence the conversation begins. It ends when she says your questions are hurting her head and you reply her answers are hurting your heart. The last voice you heard was hers. Make sure you take all your belongings with you.

You're on your own now. Single as the stars pestering the night sky. You think about the loneliness to come. You remember the loneliness you left behind. You finally admit to yourself that you were both stars at knowing how to be perfectly lonely together. You feel your heart cave in, her memory still framed and polished, still raw and imposing. You need a distraction. Music. Headphones. Shuffle. You turn the volume up. Maximum. Fuck. Coltrane. Track three. You kick the seat again but now there's nobody left to apologise to. Everyone's gone to their final destination. You take your headphones off, putting them in your rucksack. You think about dumping everything but now you've understood something about rejection. The last voice you hear is hers. This train terminates here; please ensure you have all your belongings with you when you leave the carriage.

The Blink That Killed The Eye

W e'd been split up for around three months. Since leaving I hadn't seen or heard from her and finding a decent job was proving to be a hopeless task. I had some savings in an account my father opened for me before he died, for an emergency he'd stress, but that money too was running low. At first I had nowhere to go. I thought to stay with my mum until I managed to sort myself out, but she was back to living with my step-sister in a one-bedroom apartment, so that option cancelled itself out immediately. After a week of sleeping on my cousin's futon my friend Wilton finally got back to my messages, offering me his spare room for £30 a week. I accepted, packing my few belongings then thanking my cousin for his concern and hospitality. Living with Wilton was admittedly easy but I needed my own space, somewhere I could attempt to salvage what was left of my spirit and heart. Before long l found a small room to rent on the outskirts of London. The old lady who owned the house spoke openly about her beloved dead husband and her two sons, Kevin and Matthew, both of whom had emigrated to Australia a few years back. Every afternoon she would parade framed portraits and photo albums of her boys at every stage of their life, smiling under the reminiscent glow of their childhood mischiefs. I listened, cooked us both lunch and refilled the kettle between conversations. We agreed I'd pay £50 a week until I secured work at which point the rate would return to the £70 she had initially stipulated in the advert.

At nights, after she'd gone to sleep, I'd lay on my bed listening to old jazz and folk records and reading books I'd stumbled on in the second-hand shop round the corner. Sometimes when the weight of night became too cumbersome I'd attempt to write out my own bits. My friends were all busy with their girlfriends by now. Each one settled in a serious job with gaudy aspirations of getting on the London property ladder. Talk of the ongoing recession and national unemployment dominated the news. Still, each day I sent out my applications and each day I looked at my C.V.; a throwaway aeroplane in desperate need of a pilot, an engine and a set of real wings. All my previous jobs were embarrassingly rudimentary consisting of warehouse duties, pizza delivery, security work and labouring. In the last section of my C.V., I was advised by the guy at the job centre to list some personal interests of mine. I put down how I enjoyed writing; the only thing I felt was actually worth mentioning. In my most sincere of hearts I had always wanted to become a professional writer.

Between the interchanging banality of the work I found myself involved in I managed to compile a number of short-stories and poems, all of which were celebrated by none-other than myself. Alone I lived as the ephemeral star in my bedroom, a legend in my own thinking, yet nothing I wrote seemed capable of consecrating an impression that could exceed a mere forty-eight hours. During those tedious afternoons I would take what I had written the night before down to the old lady and read her one of the stories. She would sip tea noisily over the metaphoric parts which were more considered. She would start to fidget in her chair at the precise moment I introduced important characters or brush breadcrumbs obsessively off her lap at a scene I had spent days writing and redrafting. Once I had finished she would offer an incurious grin, then as if by default, regurgitate a story about one of her two sons. I came to despise all I had written.

One afternoon at a coffee shop I asked Wilton what he thought about my latest piece. He took a long meditative drag from his roll-up cigarette, releasing the balloons of smoke then remarked how my concepts were substandard and my style of writing average. He suggested I try challenging the reader by avoiding the obvious. His advice being to hand the syntax over to the poetry; to the more sophisticated and heightened styles of language and device, conflating both the workings of the imagination with the essential narrative. He thought as it stood the story was too prosaic for his liking. Stick with what you know he said; that's how you create the best stories. He stubbed out the cigarette then headed off to work. Soon I stopped showing my writing to anyone, my confidence shattered and my self-esteem deflated. After little deliberation I thought it best to leave it all alone for a while.

As the days and nights progressed I found myself again plummeting into an insatiable depression. It's not the undesirable chaff of each hour that prompts the intermittent feelings of inadequacy, or the dragging days which influence the mind's relentless juggernaut. It's how rejection sanctifies itself into becoming a permanent feature in the way you see yourself – as the person nobody wants. Even the old lady began preferring to eat her lunches alone, claiming she had letters to write to her son Kevin whose wife was pregnant with their first child. One Tuesday afternoon I received a phone-call after having just finished skimming through a local paper. It was my cousin asking me in a hurried voice if I was still out of work. I replied I was.

'You fancy doing some part-time stuff for a charity?'

'Depends what it is and if it's paid.'

'Beggars can't be choosers mate, you want work or not? Listen, I'm driving so I can't talk but basically this charity deals with people who've got acquired brain injury.'

'Acquired brain injury?'

'Yeah.'

'What's that?'

'No idea, take down the geezer's number. Call him today. His name's Tom or Tim, something like that.'

I jotted the number down but he hung up before I could thank him. I stared at the piece of paper. Another dud lottery ticket I thought. After a few minutes I called and asked for Tom or Tim.

'We don't have anyone called Tim who works here love, who you after?'

'The general manager, I'm calling about the assistant position.'

'Oh right, then you want Tom. One second, let me call him over.' I listened as she pulled herself away from the receiver.

'Tom, there's someone on the phone here who wants to talk to you about the job they've just put up.'

'Blimey that was quick, alright one second.'

His voice sounded sprightly and affectionate. He asked if I was able to go over and meet him tomorrow afternoon for a chat, I said I would be. He called out the address as I scribbled it down on the same paper I'd written the number on. The first interview I would have had in weeks.

'So say around 3pm?' he said.

'Yep that's perfect, cheers Tom.' I replied.

'No worries mate, oh and the centre is called Mind's Eye, there's some new-builds to the left and a little organic food cafe to the right, you can't miss it. I'll see you tomorrow.'

As I made my way into the building the first thing to strike me was the overwhelming pungency of disinfectant and bleach, fused with the sharp smell of other sanitising products. The walls were all systematically painted a serene hospital-blue, with basic examples of artwork pinned up in various corners. The lighting appearing to be bright and deliberate in its artificiality. Walking hesitantly into the main space I was met by bands of people sat docilely around circular tables. Some conversed in a brusque fragmented manner, while others languidly browsed over newspapers until becoming transfixed on the final few sports pages at the back. There were those who gawked inanely out the teasing windows, their faces ravaged and inexpressive after having had any signs of happiness extirpated. Their clothing consisted of either red or blue football shirts, drab tracksuit bottoms or thin denim coats combined with long shapeless jeans and beaten trainers. If not positioned around the tables the chairs all appeared to be aligned in formal rows, as if trying to adumbrate a doctor's waiting room, the kind specifically designed to soften the poor handicap of those who for the rest of their lives will exist inside some type of physical disability. A world where unimpaired movement had now become a deceased luxury, exclusively reserved for the able-bodied and able-minded. In the corner was an old sofa, a sullen boy sat inverted playing with his fingers, a folded newspaper by his side.

As I scanned the room in a vain attempt to pick out Tom I saw how many people were in fact static, confined enduringly to their metallic wheelchairs, their lachrymose chariots, while being assisted by another person who sat upright and alert beside them. Concerned and agile, these people who I assumed were their carers seemed to be from a more familiar world. They moved around, handing out mugs of tea or water to the unresponsive posture of those rooted or bound.

There were others seated who I presumed had less obvious injuries as they appeared to be more mobile, albeit hindered by the ubiquitous postponing ghost-walk prevalent in places such as this. A semi-impediment, the kind that at some point may have known the exultancy of freedom but then subsequently found itself indignantly reduced to becoming a lagging, despondent plod. Eventually a tall casual-looking man with unafraid hair and giant working hands emerged from the kitchen waving his arms effusively. He called my name while heralding a luminosity I hadn't seen in any one for a long period of time. We shook hands. He asked if I had difficultly finding the building. I told him I hadn't. He listened faithfully as I blabbered on about a friend who lived close by while following him through into his small, cluttered office. There he briefed me on the job and the days he would need me to work.

Before coming to the interview I'd thought it best to do some research into what acquired brain injury actually was. I developed a rough idea but with the Internet being a dubious realm of unlicensed fact and conjecture, I felt it best to ask him directly. Faintly, so as not to cause offence to anyone who might be listening I asked what acquired brain injury was. With a benign teacher-like cadence he explained that it's the name given to a brain injury an individual may have incurred through an accident in later life as opposed to one conceived at birth.

'The most common causes being things such as car-crashes, gang violence, drug or alcohol abuse and incidentally people falling over.'

'Falling over?'

'Yep, they go out on the weekends, have a little too much to drink, get careless and before you know it they're on the floor. It's the prefrontal cortex that's most susceptible. Once it's damaged it causes all sorts of problems. Things like memory, coordination, speech, social interaction, decision-making and literacy all suffer. Of course all this is dependent on the severity of the fall. It's really unfortunate, when you meet the guys you'll see what I mean.'

I thought about the small cluster of folks congregated outside, hobbling and drooling their way through the day. I wanted to ask him about the young boy on the sofa playing with his fingers, what his story was, but I didn't. Opening up the files on his desk Tom continued to outline the duties I'd be required to undertake, all of which sounded purposeful and straightforward. Tasks such as assisting the members, as he called them, set up for breakfast, engage them in conversations, ask simple questions about their evening with the intention of stimulating the damaged parts of their brains and working on rebuilding cognitivity. Around midday I would join in collective exercises and activities. He gave me examples of word association games that the members enjoyed as well as bigger group activities such as charades and hangman.

'Oh and dominos, yeah they absolutely love dominos, especially Roger. He's the fella wearing the Chelsea shirt sitting by the door. Always reading the paper or doing crosswords. I don't think he's lost a game in about two years.'

At 2pm I would help prepare lunch with a small team of caterers, then at 5pm a bus would come to take some of the members back to their place of residence.

'How come they don't all get on the bus?'

'Well it depends on their mobility and how much funding they each get.'

'I see, and is it the council that funds them?'

'Yeah, depending on their injury each member receives a certain amount of financial support to come here.'

'And will this be the same group who come every day?'

'No no, most of these guys are only here once a week except Arthur who comes more or less every day. He's one of the wealthiest members we have. It would be great to have them all everyday but funding's the main issue with these things. Tomorrow will be another lot but we'll never have more than thirty people here in a day.'

'So when they're not here what do they do?'

'Some are looked after by other charities, some even have part-time jobs but for the most part I imagine they stay at their care homes or with family.'

He pulled out another few documents from his draw, running his eyes down them crossing one leg over the other before opening up the subject of pay and legality. It would be £8.50 an hour. I would take my lunch jointly with other staff and centre members. Finally he stressed I was never to be left alone with any member at any given time.

'Is that all ok?'

'Yeah sounds fine. One thing though, what's the policy with regards to asking them how they got their injury?' He stretched out in his seat, both hands cupped around the back of his head.

'It's a tricky one to be honest mate, when a new member joins us I'm given their full history, we run health checks etcetera, but can only disclose that stuff at certain times. So if you're doing one-on-one activities and they are known for having a propensity to act up, or maybe getting a bit aggressive if something sets them off then I'll give you a run down, but because you're not a qualified carer you won't be left alone with them. By law we have to allocate a supporting member of staff to shadow you, making sure you're in a space that's visible.'

'Right ok, but what happens if they decide to start telling me stuff about their accident?'

'That's totally fine. Listen, don't get me wrong, I'm just going through the official way of doing things. If you look around you'll see we're not in a usual workspace here, we're dealing with people who've suffered some real tragedies so naturally you're going to be put in positions where others might not know what to do.'

I told him I understood although I wasn't sure how I'd fare with not knowing the cause of their injuries. The interview was coming to an end, he began filing away the loose bits of paper from around his desk while I waited for questions or another snippet of information. I edged forward on my chair preparing to leave when he asked if I had any previous experience working within the mental health sector. I said honestly that I hadn't. He stabled his gaze. From the way his blue eyes pushed and contorted their way past my face excavating the more concealed depths of my character, I felt then I knew what he was searching for. Some kind of signal or sign. How my hands broke apart then came back together when I was explaining myself. The way in which I spoke. The words I used to articulate myself, but more saliently if I had within me the capacity to understand the dire situation of the people in the room next door. He was probing for the slightest inkling to gauge my levels of tolerance. Searching his gut feelings. Did I have the ability to cultivate compassion for those who were at a constant state of disadvantage? I like to believe that from somewhere within his taciturn inspection, what he unearthed in me fortified some kind of incommunicable assurance. He was, to this day, the first person who attempted to dialogue with the version of myself living beneath the name, the race, the gender and skin. Affectionately he gestured his head as I sat there immersed in trepidation and doubt.

'How are you fixed for next Monday?'

'Next Monday?' I said clearing my throat.

'Yeah, you fancy coming in and doing a trial day. At least that way you get a chance to meet everyone properly, hang out and just get a general feel for the place.'

'Yeah, that would be great.'

'Brilliant, alright mate next Monday it is. Oh, remember to bring your passport and an old utility bill. I need to make photocopies. Legal stuff.'

'Yeah no worries, what time you want me here for?'

'10am.'

'Ok cool, I'll see you then.'

Walking back through the main lounge area I tried to acknowledge each member with a smile, nobody seemed to notice me though. Lost in their own worlds, one I was just approaching. I turned to the sofa to see if the young boy was still playing with his fingers but the space was vacant, the newspaper still unread and folded on the side.

The following Monday the members arrived a few minutes after I did. The bus pulled up outside the building parking with its hazard lights blinking against the curb. Wheelchairs were cautiously manoeuvred onto the pavement by men wearing frayed high-visibility vests. I watched on from the windows of the kitchen.

'They're a great bunch, they really are,' Tom said, a half-buttoned flannel shirt exposing the top part of his chest. I felt cold and stiff but he looked hot, active and alive. He filled a big white bowl with plain cereal using a giant glass pitcher to pour in the semi-skimmed milk.

'Yeah I know it's grim but it's either this or toast I'm afraid. Liam who I'll introduce you to brings in his own food, and Janet who's Abdullah and Rosemary's carer sorts their breakfast and lunch. You fancy getting the tea ready? Sugar is over there, tea-bags under here, dash all the dirty spoons into the Tupperware by the sink.' He could see the panic setting in, everything becoming increasingly overwhelming. How would I speak to them? How would I introduce myself? Who am I? What am I doing here? What do I do? What have I done? What if they hate me? What if I mess something up and someone gets hurt or upset?

'Shit, sorry dude, I know I'm just throwing loads of stuff at you but if there's anything you don't understand or you're not sure about just ask ok? I'll point out who's who once we're all settled in. We should have roughly fifteen today so a nice number to get started with.'

I poured hot water into the giant pot with two tea bags inside, sitting nervously around the table waiting for the first batch of members to arrive. The second flux of trepidation made wires out of my insides. Would I remember their names? How did they end up here? What were they like before their accident? How old were they? Did they believe in God? Were they atheists? Agnostics? How do they deal with their injury? Do they get lonely? Since a boy I'd become averse to being around disabled people and children for long periods of time, a problem I was more than aware of but didn't dare tell Tom. Despite their low-ranking level within society there was something profoundly free about both those kind of people, which for someone who's always lived with the constant feeling of restraint and fear can be intimidating.

'Hello my love, you must be Alex? I'm Janet.' She extended a sweaty open hand, the other brushing aside the strands of white hair beginning to slyly colonise regions of her head where her natural black once grew.

'This your first day is it?'

'Yeah.'

'Don't look so worried darling, by the end of the day you'll be wanting to take em' all home with you.'

A raspy chuckle followed; the youth of her face appearing to have expired long ago but the strength in her eyes still determined to preserve the hope she had somewhere found. Taking a silver flask out from her bag she poured hot coffee into a cup, the steam and aroma trailing lazily upwards.

'You alright for tea?'

'Yeah I'm good thanks, just made some,' pointing to the pot on the table.

'Great stuff, getting stuck in already. Tom said it's your first time working with disabled people?'

'Yeah, I don't really know what to expect.'

'Ahh, they're a super lot, they really are.' Squinting out towards the parked bus she said, 'you see that fella there in the wheelchair, that's Arthur. If he don't make you want to come back next week, nothing will.'

Walking off she laughed again, more sizeably this time, taking a sharp sip of coffee then going over to the table to lay the outstanding pieces of cutlery for breakfast.

They entered the lounge. Those in wheelchairs came in first, their carers behind pushing cautiously. Those more supple ambled in a few moments later. Two went straight over to the pool table, setting up a rack of multicoloured balls. Another guy with a bright jacket and an oversized baseball cap plugged his music device into the centre's stereo system. I looked to see if the boy who had been sitting on the sofa last week would make a return but there was no sign of him.

'Sammy, sorry mate, can we lower it down just a tad? It's maybe a bit too early for another Brooklyn Hammer session. You can turn it up after the games later, alright?' Tom's voice boomed from somewhere inside the kitchen, a reminder that he was in charge. The youngster unplugged his device with snapping indignation, settling down instead to watch the other two boys start their game of pool. From first glance they couldn't have been much older than twenty yet on closer inspection there was an obvious age disparity. Why were there also more men than women? I thought back to what Tom had said about being drunk and falling over. I wondered what the official statistics were. Was acquired brain injury more common among men?

Maybe there's more women on a Tuesday, or a Wednesday. Maybe the country was being run by a bunch of sexist pigs or maybe this was all in my head.

'Hi nice to meet you are you new here or a member here today is it your first time here or are you new today?' By the time she got to the end of the sentence her oversized glasses were already dipping down towards the lower end of her nose. Her skin looked aggressively scarred and flakey. My guess was that she was around eighteen. She had a surplus of foaming saliva collating around the corners of her mouth, her teeth morosely forgotten. I replied in the same awkward way a person might when attempting to communicate with someone whose understanding of English is minimal, affirming bluntly that I was not a member but it was my first day. My breathing grew heavier with my throat tightening up. My nerves brimmed uncontrollably.

'Esi, this is Alex.'

'Alex. Alex, is he a member here please or is he working here with you and Janet and Suki?'

'Hopefully he'll be working with us a few days a week.' Tom had come up from behind reiterating what I had said but with more tact, resting a brotherly arm on my shoulder.

'Janet's put your breakfast out Esi, why don't you go over and sit with the others. You remember what happened on Friday? There was no cereal left by the time you got round to eating. You have to be quick..go..go..go!'

He clapped and shuffled his feet, playfully signifying for her to hurry up. She laughed noisily then turned to waddle away with the footsteps of a child, taking her seat alone over at the far end of breakfast table.

'What's wrong with her?' I asked invectively.

'Nothing's wrong with her. She can feel, she understands, she thinks, cries, laughs and gets angry, just like us. She just does things a bit differently, in their own order, that's all.'

For a split second his phrasing reminded me of my father, a revolving sensation filling my heart, I missed him. There was no blame in Tom's voice. He'd probably had umpteen idiots like me pose the same ignorant question. With another reassuring pat on the back he went over to join the other members at the table. A green sticker on the wall pointed to where the male toilets were. I needed to wash my hands.

'Alex,' Tom called as I dried my hands down the side of my jeans, 'come sit yourself down over here. There's somebody we want you to meet.'

He was the oldest member at Mind's Eye, the years having thoroughly traversed the pale skin of his face, his hair meagre and balding. He sat disarranged and hunched, entombed within the barriers of his wheelchair, his hands acting as a claw-like glove where each finger in its own frozen suffering screamed for release, like a set of distorted antennas each pointing in opposing directions. Like he had been struck obscenely by this paralysis at the exact moment his life reached out to point the way towards the route it wished to forever take. His body deprived of its own body. Everything out of bounds. No satisfaction, no rage, no physical love, a man trapped brutally within the cage of himself. His spectacles may have been the same ones he'd worn his entire life and a plain blue shirt and stained corduroy trousers helped to conceal the elephantine mounds of his body's muscular dystrophy. He, like Esi, appeared to be perpetually afflicted by the same tiny blots of clinging saliva around the mouth. Looking at the other members I saw how each person, each mouth, seemed to uniformly house these thick deposits of white spittle. Maybe it was the medication? Were they aware? Shouldn't somebody tell them or wipe them clean? Didn't their carers find it foul? A lady sat endearingly beside him. Astute and benevolent she tucked a paper napkin into his shirt, lifting the cereal bowl up towards his mouth until he was chewing his breakfast in a halcyon, motorised way. Some of the members looked like people you would expect to find in a supermarket or shopping centre, other's looked like they constantly needed the care and attention of somebody else. Again I could feel my mind drifting off, trying to morbidly picture the kind of accident they would have been involved in. What misfortune had found the Achilles' heel of their destiny, striking them down with such enormity and vengeance? Again, why were they here?

'He just said good morning to you.'

I pretended not to hear, unsure as to whether the statement was directed at me or at somebody else. I reached over for the glass pitcher to pour a little more milk into my second cup of tea. Stirring, trying my best to look distracted.

'Hey Mr. Alex. He said good morning to you.'

'Oh. Oh did he? Sorry, I didn't hear. Good morning…?'

'Arthur. This is Arthur Harding.'

'Oh, good morning Arthur Harding, I've heard some wonderful things about you.'

It was false. Condescending. Of course it was. The only thing this man was capable of doing was moving his eyes and mouth back and forth in a struggling anthem of inaudible murmurs and faint signals, yet even he could tell how contrived my question was.

'He said he's upset,' she said casually.

'Is he? I'm sorry to hear that. Why are you upset Arthur?'

I was speaking to a grown man, a man whose years clearly surpassed mine yet I was speaking to him as he if was a child. I could hear it, the simple infantilizing pitch entrenched in my voice, mastering my tongue. At that moment an awful cloud of futility came over me, what a terrible way to start a new job I thought. I'm not cut out for all this shit. I'm full of judgment and preconception. This isn't how it should be. Maybe I'll tell Tom this wasn't such a great idea after all. I'll say I don't have enough experience in the field of mental health. That my temperament is off. Then I thought of the old lady and the rent. My money running out.

'Because he has to have Muesli again.'

'What?' I snapped unexpectedly.

'He's upset because he has to have Muesli again,' her voice oblivious to the irascibility in mine.

'I don't understand, what's wrong with Muesli?'

The group all burst into a fit of laughter as if it were the particular humour of their revered leader, a joke emanating from the great beacon of all their hopes.

'Well maybe we can ask Tom to prepare something

different for tomorrow,' I said, my face stuck somewhere between the discomfort of embarrassment and the failed attempt of trying to outsmart a more confident group. Nothing. Not even a slight giggle. Every muscle in Arthur's face remained locked, taking influence from some far-off stone or a piece of dead earth. She lifted up a spoonful of white milk mixed with soggy bits of floating cereal but Arthur's mouth joined the rest of his face, remaining obstinately cemented. He didn't want to eat.

'Oh God, now he needs to wee,' his carer declared exasperatingly.

'To wee? How do you know?' I asked.

'The same way you and I know. We just feel it.'

'You feel it for him?'

'I feel it for him,' she laughed approvingly.

Getting up she unlocked the brakes from the bottom of the wheelchair and wheeled him out, almost as if he was now a piece of wooden furniture, one being moved from one part of the room to another. I remained staring at the rippling assimilation of milk and cereal they had left in front of me. The silver spoon dumped carelessly on the table, smeared with the loose flakes of skin from his dry mouth, tarnishing its famous silver gleam.

Refilling a jug of water and placing it on the table Tom sat down to say, 'Arthur's our oldest member. That's Suki his carer, lovely lovely lady. I've been here for nearly five years. When I joined he'd already been coming to the centre for six. He's a veteran and a real character when you get to know him, although he'll take a bit of getting used to…as most of us do.' I nodded my head in understanding.

'I don't get it. How does she know? His carer, Suki, how can she just tell when he needs to go to the loo?'

'You don't have children do you?'

I didn't. I told him how I had split from my girlfriend three months ago and was renting a room in the old lady's house.

'Oh right, well I'm sorry to hear about the break up. I don't have kids either but my brother does. Chester's his name. They come round our house for dinner on Sundays. My girlfriend and I cook the old traditional roast with all the trimmings. Chester's two right, he sits up at the table in his highchair splatting out this mess of sounds. Some of the stuff he says is actually pretty interesting if you're into phonetics. Me and my brother think it's brilliant, but his wife Amali, she just turns round and says something like, 'no that's too hot, don't give him that' or 'he's tired now, he's needs more water, he prefers the mash.' Me, Mike and Vicky are left looking at her like how the hell do you do that? You see it everywhere. Even people with their pets or with their flowers in the gardens. Some kind of weird intuition takes over, nobody else can see or feel it apart from you but it's definitely real.'

I could see why Tom was suited for looking after the members at Mind's Eye. Why he had scanned my humanity in such a punctilious way on the afternoon of my interview. From what I could tell he had this remarkable and rare ability to simply let people be, always looking for ways to celebrate the good in a world where so much had already gone wrong. To not judge the fault inside the human but rather to understand the human inside the fault.

'You said you like writing didn't you?'

'I did. Well I do. I, just … not so much my own stuff anymore.'

'Really, why's that?'

'I don't know. I can't seem to write anything I like for longer than a few hours. I read other people's work and it leaves me with this feeling of inadequacy if you know what I mean.'

He looked around the room to check nobody needed anything. The boys were still engrossed in their game of pool, with the younger member patiently looking on. Arthur's muesli waited for his return, Esi poured herself another cup of tea. I envisioned myself coming to work here each day, learning the stories and temperaments of each person and for once the wires that churned away in my stomach began an attempt at untangling themselves.

'So you compare your writing to others?'

'I guess so, but we all do. Compare ourselves I mean. I don't think it's something we do deliberately, but then there's no real other way we can move forward. We see what others have or where they are and we use that as a way to measure our own progression. I don't know how healthy it all is though.'

'Yeah, but we forget that people are like gamblers.'

'How you mean?'

'Well, they only really want you to see how much they've won and never how much they've had to lose in order to win.'

Again it was something I could imagine my father saying. The difference being that Tom's insight came from a place of practice rather than from a place of bitterness and detachment. My father always choosing to share his musings from the deep privacy of his small room whereas Tom was here finding ways to implement everything he believed, after all a philosophy which can't be applied to life is nothing but a series of well-formed ramblings.

'So can we be here without comparison do you think?'

'I don't think so,' he sighed, rubbing his index finger around the rim of his coffee cup.

'I'm not claiming to have all the answers but I know how difficult it can be to see where others are in such a rigid social system. A system really based on privilege, status and visibility which becomes really frustrating when you relate it back to your own situation and progression like you said, but that's all counterproductive. To put it another way, if you're comparing something as unique and personal as life or writing or any kind of subjective art then it's like trying to compare the fracture of two people's hearts. Like trying to distinguish a commonality in the way hearts break. We all know nothing breaks in exactly the same place right? We all hurt and express those feelings in a language that distinguishes us from the next person. You shouldn't undermine your work just because it doesn't sound as articulate or sophisticated as another writer's. Everything works in its own way but that doesn't mean it's not coming from a place of sincerity. My mum was a writer believe it or not, well, a hobbyist rather than a professional but she would tell me and my brother that there's always profundity, even in nothingness. I realised the same thing working here with people nobody wanted to listen to, people who are socially void of any real attention. The way they share their experiences is what some might call simple or child-like, but there's courage in sharing the things that hurt us, in the revealing of secrets. Sorry one second mate.'

He rose from his seat quickly, hurrying over towards the toilet to see if Arthur and Suki needed assistance. When he came back slightly out of breath he asked if I wanted some more tea, before I could reply he was already filling up my cup.

'I get what you're saying, I've just never been the kind to share those sort of things before, I find it difficult. A while back I performed some poems at an open-mic night, but then I didn't know anyone there and you don't need bravery to show a bunch strangers where it hurts.'

'You'll be surprised, the human experience isn't exclusive to just you Alex. Hopefully by you being here it'll open you up to a different kind of story. Take all those folks outside, they get up every morning to a routine consisting mainly of some text-book activities, light physiotherapy, plain food and maybe some television. That's life. Day in and day out. The most upsetting part about the whole thing is many of them still remember what it was like to live without a brain injury. I often think what it must be like to still recall those times, the ones where you danced at a party, exercised, went for long walks. They were like us once, sitting here discussing similar things with all their senses intact, now they're completely reliant on others. Still you see them here, talking, persevering. You want courage Alex, look in the places where we're taught not to look. The unlit corners. The places where the magazines close their pages. Where journalists put away their notepads. Where people keep walking on. Where the cameras run out of battery and the reporters suddenly lose their voice. There's courage in this world, it's just not always where you'd expect to find it. That's what I've come to realise anyway.'

He took the final sip of his tea as if pulling himself out from his thoughts, thoughts that surpassed general theory and were instead steeped ardently in his every-day life along with the offerings he made to others.

'I was thinking, seeing as Arthur's a big fan of writing how would you feel about spending the morning with him? You can just run through some simple activities, word association games, memory exercises, that kind of thing?'

Instantly I felt a wave of apprehension ricochet through my body, around my stomach and up into the palate of my mouth. All our lofty talk on courage was suddenly shattered by a reality I felt unfit to face. I was robbed of speech, of sound, my hands frozen in their very palms. I felt like him. Like Arthur. For a fleeting but essential moment I thought I felt the stasis of his dusty veins.

'I'll set the table up in the activities room,' he said, slapping a hand across my knee.

'The other's can stay out here. I think we're going to be finishing off the paper masks we started last week anyway. It's for this little play we're putting on at the mayor's fair next month. You won't need pens and paper for Arthur but there's a whiteboard in there if you want to use it. Suki will be with you so if you have trouble understanding him she'll be able to help.'

We headed over to the activities room. Tom was alive and the more time I spent with him the more I realised how dead I had been. In the activity room he wiped down the random drawings on the board handing me a set of different coloured markers. With one last assuring pat on the back he left the room as Arthur and Suki slowly entered.

'Oh he loves this writing stuff, it's one of his favourite things. You best have your words ready Mr. Alex, Arthur takes no prisoners.' She laughed heartily while wheeling him over into the light. The morning sun pounced through the slits of the room's metallic blinds, filling the space with the warm translucent shards of light, the delicate life-blood of everything. I sat next to him. He must have been in his mid thirties although he looked much older. A few stubborn flakes of cereal hanging onto the bristles of his beard.

'So you like words Arthur?' I said, 'you want to play some games to see how good you are?' My mind lobbed itself back to those primary school days. Quickly I put together a few uncomplicated exercises in my head, ones that wouldn't encumber a mind such as his.

'Why not?' she asked him, 'Arthur, you remember how much fun we had on Friday playing word games with Adrian and Shameela? Come on don't be like this now.'

'What's wrong?' I said enquiringly.

'It looks like he doesn't want to write today. He's saying he only enjoys it when the weather's bad and today, well, it's too sunny.'

Imagine what it would sound like if a stone were to try and open its mouth and speak. How it would articulate all the things it had seen and felt over millennia; its tone arid, heavy and solemn. A stone such as that could replace perfectly the grating voice of Arthur Harding. His incomprehensible stuttering was like a drill ramming itself suicidally into the marrow of a wall. A brick wall. The thought transported me back to my uncle's old building site. I wondered if he had finished that extension yet. If he was still having trouble finding the right nails for the tarpaulin. Then I thought of the storms, all of them. Then of her. My stomach stabbing itself repeatedly with its own disgust. Shaking myself from out of the stupor I asked, 'Ok, so what does he want to do then?'

'He want's to talk. He seems to be in a very talkative mood today.'

'Fine, let's talk.'

'There you go Arthur, Mr. Alex said we can talk.' His body twitched ever so slightly leaving me to assume this was the only way he could possibly express excitement. She took a cloth from her pocket wiping the strings of drool from around his mouth.

'He wants to know where you live and what you like doing.'

With a faint sigh I put the lid back on the board-marker, neatening the pile of lined paper in front of me. Rolling the marker through my fingers I replied to his question in the best way I could.

'I live on the outskirts of London. I'm twenty-six years old and all my life I've wanted to be a writer, although it's the only thing that completely terrifies me.'

He hawked out a senseless burst of impotent vowels and

consonants. He sounded like a tool-box being emptied abruptly of all its contents.

'He said you look older than twenty-six,' Suki reiterated. I tried to understand what he was saying for myself, without her, but everything felt dead by the time it reached his throat. Arthur Harding resembled someone who had once happened, who had once lived but had never managed to have the proof of that life documented. Now he was stuck here in front of me, deep inside his own life, one irrepressibly sad and opaque.

'He wants to see your hands,' Suki stated.

'My hands?'

'Yes, he wants to see them. Hold them out.'

I obliged him. Putting the marker-pen down I held out both my hands raising them up to face him. It's strange what we notice when other people take an obscure fascination in those supposedly ordinary parts of our body. The parts we never seem to consider much. Our hands. Our legs. Our arms. I found myself stretching out each individual finger, taking pride in the definitive showcase of ability. Of nail, of fist, of bone, of knuckle and dexterity. Of freedom. Of choice and strength. I turned them over. Slowly. Delighting in my vanity and over the fact I, at last, had something somebody else wanted. I revealed to him my great wide palms: unabashed, clean and loaded with all the splendid highways of the future, up until the point he began to weep. When a person whose life has been whittled down to nothing more than a heap of muscle-mass begins to cry because of your own insensitive doing, you will not know how to act. His face remained expressionless. There were no obvious creases or subversions of lamentation. The contours maintaining themselves with the heed of a trained gymnast but with his eyes softening to flicker until they erupted like geysers, a series of long, transparent, inarticulate tears massacring what was. I was abbreviated into a dungeon of guilt and despair, being left to brood on such an incendiary compulsion. Snapping back my hands, realising how I'd relished such a moment, I shamefully mumbled an apology.

'Don't be silly, don't be silly, no harm done Mr. Alex. He's happy for you, he is. You have the ability to use your hands as you wish. To write, to eat, to wash yourself, to pick up a cup of tea and blow it until it cools. Unfortunately our dear Arthur cannot. This is why he cries. He loves reading from his electronic reader,' she pulled out a small little tablet from inside a backpack attached to his wheelchair.

'He reads and reads all day, but gradually that too becomes difficult.'

She wiped his mouth with another tissue. I could see every version of myself mirrored in the tears he was crying – the only things vigorous about him. I looked on as a student might while his teacher goes on to explain the workings of a complex problem. The anguish of his indelible face, one whose only wish would be to converse and express with the world everything it had been ordered to mutely observe. I was beginning to understand the little worlds and what the lines patterning his forehead were trying to spell out. I could see beyond the horrid boulders that burdened his stature. Each one authentically conceived during moments of unspeakable sorrow, moments such as this. I could see him.

'How long have you been like this? Living this way?'

I looked at him directly. My question aimed to find not his infamous impairment but rather his prevailing vein of human. The side of him that's withstanding and courageous. The side which once ran and screamed and relished and dreamed. I was going into forbidden territory with all reasoning unconcernedly escaping me. I thought of Tom and his earlier instructions. It was too soon, but then I thought if I couldn't speak plainly to those who society relegated and dissolved to the class of the insignificant then I wouldn't want to speak to anyone at all. Never again – I would leave and return to my own wrecking penumbras engendered by the transparency I myself majored in.

'He's been here since the centre opened. That's when he had his accident, on the eve of the same year,' Suki said.

'How did it happen Arthur?' I asked.

My voice turned investigative. Cutting and detached. With everything I had learnt about acquired brain injury it was clear that someone or rather something had wantonly robbed Arthur Harding of all his prosperous years, ones he was rightfully entitled to as any human was. His glory years. He could have been a writer, a commentator, a poet, a Dickens or Tolstoy. I could have been here reading his work, his mind and musings without having to satisfy my curiosity with an eidetic image of a man who never was.

'She's right, it was New Year's Eve. Most people end up here either from alcohol or fighting, Tom's probably already told you that. I was never really a troublemaker, I was the more feeble kind of renegade. You ever been in a car crash?'

'No.'

'It's a strange situation to find yourself in. One minute you're driving along, singing with your pals, feeling good, the next everything falls silent. You can't recognise where the pain's coming from nor have you ever felt pain of that kind, but you're aware of it, you know its there which is a good thing because it tells you you're not dead. You're relived, laying there listening to yourself breathe. Car alarm sound. In your ears. You never stop hearing that. The last bits of broken glass fall from the car windows to the floor, like drops of solid rain. You hear broken sounds; deformed metal trying to reconfigure itself, pressed and squashed you try and open your eyes. Everything's upside down. Rain and blood. You can't feel anything, but you can hear.'

'We were spoilt. My mum once said we were rich boys storming into our own golden graves. Mums are overlooked prophets. My friend Tarik, his dad just bought him a new car. A Porsche, a monster of a machine. He'd only been driving a few months. He'd done a couple lines at the party we were leaving from but it was the booze ... the booze caused the crash. We were leaving one house party and heading up the A1 to another. They think he fell asleep at the wheel. Closed his eyes for a few seconds. Blinked. From then on I don't have any real recollection. It's all in drabs. I remember the road turning dark. The street- lights fading, my guess is he veered off down some country lane, that's where they found us. Those kind of nights are made for dying – cold and empty with nothing in-between. The music was turned up. Then it went black for the longest time I've ever known. The other two, Tarik and his mate Andrew both died on impact. Four fire engines. Two ambulances and four police cars. I didn't find that out until six months later.'

'Why six months?'

'I was in a coma. When I came through the only thing I could move was what you're looking at now. There's something horrible in being asleep for all that time then waking up to find out it was the cause of all your despair. The death of my friends. The brain injury. Everything. Because Tarik closed his eyes for a few seconds we all went blind forever.'

'So, how do you deal with it, the frustrations, the torment?'

'I spend time thinking about eyes. Sometimes it helps, other times it drives me mad.'

'Why eyes?'

'Because people will never fully appreciate how much work they're forced to do when all other ways of communication get stolen from you. How quick someone like me learns to become grateful for the space and light between each and every blink. I read that on average the human eye blinks fifteen thousand times a day during the time we're awake. Since my accident the only thing I can do is think how much life I lose to those little blinks, it's like each one becomes the eye's own dagger, robbing it from the only bit of remaining satisfaction, purposefully barricading the portal to the human world. If I didn't have to blink I'd be able to see it all.'

I could almost picture him now outside the grip of his injury. Almost. Everything functioning as it should be. The two of us in a bar, drinking as friends, exchanging stories while the world around us continued to happen. I would ask him if he wanted another beer. He would say yes and we would drink until nothing else could make sense.

'If you want to know the truth, which I think you do, before I ended up here I wasn't a nice person. I was rich and like most rich people I was an arsehole. My dad set me up with a small property company. After uni he bought me a three-bedroom house, said I could do what I wanted with it so I started renting it out to some students. With the money I made I bought another. Houses were cheap back then, not like now. Within a year the council had built another university campus in the area, so by the time I was twenty four I had offices, cars and over a dozen properties under my name.'

'But I thought Suki told me you were a writer? Tom said the same too.'

'No, I liked writing, I still do but it was nothing more than a stupid pipe-dream. By the time of the crash I was already addicted to it all – the rush I mean. Making money, spending it, squandering it, then having to make it all back again. I've been around the world, seen sunsets capable of making the imagination cry. I've done stuff others will always dream of but the best years of my life have been in this shitty wheelchair, disabled and reduced to being a spectator. Take Suki for instance, I never knew people like her existed. I mean, I knew but I didn't know.'

He cleared his throat. I could envision him rubbing at the crust around his lips, straightening up his posture, even lifting himself out of his wheelchair and walking over to the window. Suki appeared to be preoccupied with her phone, sending texts while I kept my stare on him.

'Today I just wanted to talk, we don't do enough of it, well we talk but mainly it's about others rather than for others. I see everyone on their smart phones, their laptops, engrossed in the digital world. It's like we're told to keep looking down missing everything which happens above. Here's a commonly asked question Alex, and please you don't have to answer if you don't want to but…do you believe in God?'

'No. All that finished a long time ago. I used to be religious but I reckon my understanding of God changed when I started to see the world for what it was. Everywhere religion's gone it's caused conflict and division, but you only see that once you look past the dogma and icons.'

'Absolutely, and you could argue the same about places religion hasn't gone, either way I've been thinking a lot about this idea of God lately, probably because I'm getting older. Not the standard figure we find in monotheistic religions but the alternative God; the one we aren't taught to fear and venerate, the invisible God that's far more present than the one depicted in mainstream scripture. How I see it is we're all addicted to some kind of deity, or to an idea of divination at least. It's all done in the hope of finding some salvation outside of ourselves, after all, we know how dark and frightening our mind's can become. When I was growing up I saw the God of the rich living in the gleam of their sports car, the grandeur of their homes, in their unnecessary opulence. A poor person's God lives far away, somewhere between a prayer and heaven, or as a figment of hope, hidden from anything seen or fathomed – the abstract God which religion tries to define in absolutist terms. The poor person's God stays unknown until the end and even then there's nothing to suggest the figure will reveal itself, but by that point the struggles of life have reached fruition, death absolves us all and religion gets repackaged and resold to another vulnerable epoch. It's unwise to speculate on death as it's unwise to speculate on a world a thousand years from now, yet at the moment of our end consciousness and intelligence as we know it ceases to give life to this imagination of ours, which essentially spawns the very ideas which divide us – ideas such as race, religion, class and nationality are products of human thought and intelligence, abstract entities which require the human mind to espouse them. The irony being we're all searching for the same thing just in different places and in different ways. We fight, we wage wars, we systematically ruin the lives of others, we create systems of supremacy and wealth, we control, we dominate, we pillage and all this is fuelled by our own agonising despair. Now I'm here talking to you from the inside, living totally dependant on Suki, the same person who I would have probably insulted and abused in some miserable way before my accident. Now my body calls on her body and strength for its activity, my voice has become her voice and my life each day relies on hers for sustenance. This is the stuff I ponder on when everyone goes home. It would be a lie to say when I think about it all, it didn't hurt.'

Suki looked up, putting her phone back into her handbag.

'Mr. Alex, are you ok?' she asked.

'Yes, sorry, I zoned out for a second. Does he have any more questions?'

'I'm sure he does, he likes you I can tell. Arthur my love, do you want more tea? Come on, we can come back when it's raining to do our writing with Mr. Alex. He's not always this quiet, usually he has lots to say, especially to new people, I hope he's not getting ill again.'

'It's probably because he's not used to me. Can I ask, what's it like being his interpreter?'

'His interpreter? I've never thought of it like that. That sounds very grand,' she chuckled, 'For me personally I don't see it in such a way though.'

Rolling out his wheelchair she put her small frame into his entire determinant, into every side of his paralysis and helplessness.

'How do you see it then?' I asked, not expecting her to answer.

She stopped pushing, as if taken aback by the question, or maybe by the inquisitiveness I was showing in an area, that for her, always existed in its own thankless vacuum.

'Nobody's ever asked me that before. For me Mr. Alex this is a human obligation and if you ask me why I see it that way, I would have to dig a little deeper to answer you.'

'Maybe because we're all human together, at the same time, and we're all interdependent on one another for survival?' I added, trying to encourage her to reveal more about her dedication to Arthur.

'Yes, perhaps you're right. Now, can I ask you something quite personal Mr. Alex?'

'Sure, oh and please Alex is fine, no need for the mister.'

'Ok, Alex then. Have you ever seen anyone die?'

'No. No, haven't.'

'And I hope you never have to. Because those last few moments which swallow up a person, someone who has lived, who was once alive, who may have had children or had given their hours to building a career and providing for their family can never be shaken off. Someone who is loved by someone else. Who has perhaps raised children to be fine and decent people. Someone who has learned to love and has lost love. A person needed. A person seen, known. Then, within the snap of a finger, the pull of a trigger, they're gone. Forever. The only endings worth celebrating are the ones which manage to champion their beginnings, but where I come from those stories are few and far between.'

She was in the same place as Tom was earlier, the place he'd forgotten himself in, the place that inspired people like them to wake up each morning and devote yet another day to help better another person's life.

'I hope you don't mind me talking about this,' she said softly.

'Not at all, this morning was for talking after all,' I declared.

'The first time you see someone die you're not too sure what's happening. You feel the softest parts of their body, the part you loved to hold and cuddle in times of trouble become as hard as the table top you're resting on. You're forced to watch them become nothing but a struggling morsel in the ancient mouth of death, and a gluttonous death it is Alex. Then the blood begins to leave the exit wound like a terrible magic trick. And the blood flows like sewage from a leaking pipe, the blood they spent so long trying to preserve. To nourish. To feed life into. His wasn't a natural death, my husband's, it was murder. Murdered blood does not mix well with the parched earth Alex – I don't know if you know that. It's meant to remain within the body, it's not designed for the arteries of the ground. All you can do is wail and call out but to the arrival of nothing or no one. The soldiers have done their killing for the day. The politicians have peddled their polished speeches of peace and negotiations but on the killing field there are no ambulances. No white flags. No doctors, just a fire so hot you can burn your very eyes on it, and carnage, the long valley of carnage. No news reporters. No aid. No soundbite. No documentaries or placards for protests, just a poor death you learn to haul in silence for the rest of your life. It leaves such an impression on you that the only way you can assuage its demon is by doing everything within your power to make sure nobody else has to suffer even slightly the same way again. So you give. You don't take, you keep giving. You delve into this; into helping and being there when nobody else wants to be.'

She pulled a tissue out from the back of her jean pocket, the same pack she used to dry Arthur's eyes twenty minutes ago, letting the tears fall and become absorbed by its whiteness. Wheeling him out of the room she stopped and leaned closer into him.

'I don't know Arthur. He might not be comfortable with that kind of thing.'

'Be comfortable with what?' I called out.

She turned to me. Her eyes still lodged inside the

memory of a pain they only seconds ago laid bare.

'He wants you to show him where you hurt.'

Rising from my seat I walked over to him. Kneeling down beside the thin rubber wheel of his chair I took his intractable fingers, bringing them up to the side of my head to meet the fine details of a scar just above my right ear – my single belonging. The one thing she let me keep. I moved his hand, helping him navigate along its crooked width and breadth, as if it were the permanent chalk-line to a murder I once witnessed, one I could only ever talk to about with a man such as Arthur.

'What are you doing?' Suki asked.

'Giving something back, like you said.'

'He can't feel anything. Movement wasn't the only thing that died on the day of his accident, his nervous system went too.'

'I reckon we're all capable of feeling something slightly more profound if given the right chance, even if we can't bring ourselves to show it.'

I returned Arthur's fingers back to the armrests of his wheelchair when in that moment I felt an almost invisible push happen against my hand and wrist. He was resisting, standing up for all the silent maladies life had inflicted on everyone like him. He was opposing those prejudices, those stigmas, those presuppositions in such a clandestine way but with enough force for me to feel it push up against my blood. To recognise its pulse. With only the slightest bit of strength his hand declared itself a part of mine, like the way a fallen leaf might do when gently brushing into another during the sweep of a cold autumn wind. I looked him in the eyes the way Tom had looked at me only last week. His face still unswerving and ineffectual. I wanted him to speak as loud as I knew he could. To scream. To fucking jump and sing and share his golden philosophies on people and life and religion. I wanted him to tell Suki all the things he'd told me. How he loved her and how he was eternally thankful for everything she did. I wanted him to tell her the things I'm sure he told me. To bring out the crowns of all the worlds he'd kept locked inside him. I'd discovered an entire universe trapped in a wheelchair and I couldn't bare the thought of him taking all that with him down into a lonely grave. But he didn't jump. He didn't sing. Or speak. Or move. As always, nothing happened. A reel of clear dribble dangled from his mouth, like an impractical bit of web the spider will in due course come to disregard. She took out another tissue and wiped his mouth, stroking the back of his head.

Suki wheeled Arthur Harding out into the main lobby where he rejoined his group of men and women. They were getting ready to rehearse for the Mayor's show next month. Their papier-mâché masks pulled over their heads, as if secretly wanting to disguise the features of their true face. Men and women who were once endowed with the common privilege of health and independence, but who were now forced to depend on the philanthropy and understanding of those more able. Those who in their own courageous way were also fighting some long and concealed war.

The next morning I called Tom to tell him I wasn't going to be returning to Mind's Eye. He said it wouldn't be a problem, thanking me for letting him know. He suggested I have another go at writing again. The last thing I remember him saying was he understood.

Last Lament

I will die on a Thursday. Mid-November, in my seventy-eighth year. At the discovery of my body I will have been dead for nearly two days, then, the room will be cleaned and fumigated. Within a week a new advert will appear in the same newspaper I purchased all those years ago, with the sole intention of finding a cheaper, more private style of accommodation after my wife and I separated.

It will have just gone 4pm and the school children outside will be filling the narrow pavements with the momentous avidity reserved for all things undiscovered and waiting. I will think of my son and the conversations we shared. I will see his face grinning and wild at first, then grimaced and melancholy in the years to follow. A cup of tea will be by my bedside, cold and half-finished in its spectral stasis. The weather will be unforgiving and dark as is to be expected from such a cantankerous season.

I will have the window open slightly. The heating turned up. Inside, the room will consist of my few possessions, ones with enough sentimental recall that they could each act as a singular map documenting the non-sequential course of my life's journey. There will be books. The muted instruments I acquired in those demented attempts to pacify my curiosity for all things human or dead. To excavate the meaning of the words life and to live. To understand the brutal nature of death while still being cradled by its grand antithesis. Within those oxidising pages there will be characters which had me weeping at the turn of their demise, or becoming alive at the successive unveiling of their amorous affairs. There will be pages loaded with unequivocal facts, which helped me to make sense of the injustices done by one to another. Those inflicted by the whites onto the poor backs of the blacks. Those inflicted by the whites onto the poor backs of the brown and those inflicted by the whites onto the poor backs of the whites.

There will be a plethora of polemics, ones that upon a day now gone would stare back at me, as I read satiating my mind with the fury of their nailing knowledge, leading me deeper into circles charged with opinion and ego. Where ego trumped opinion and opinion lived irrespective of fact. Books that caused me to send their pages hurling against the wall of my home, and yes there will be poetry. Words that broke my heart just to prove I could still live through their agonies. Verses in orthodox form, in free form, villanelles, haikus, sonnets and cantos. In ballads and limericks, or odes and quatrains, all of which had me repeating lines throughout nights when my very bones felt like burning wood in some besieged forest. Names of my most favoured and loved authors will scramble my thinking. Sesquipedalian and prodigious, their language and their characters live nestled in an impenetrable place within. And there will be music. A portable archive of records and songs that rocked me weightless in each testing period of my life. The electric pulse of the guitar in all its tenets. The gulping blues, the restless jazz of the oppressed and destitute, the averse folk songs opening gates to the sleeping gardens of my imagination. These will be neatly arranged in a pile below my books, with the insurmountable precision of an old watch-maker who has now grown tired of time.

Then, in the mantelpiece of my heart, close to where I'll keep all the memories of those who gave my life its breath, will be a list of names with frozen, still faces. I will think back to my wife and wonder what name now grows within the fondness of her heart. To the women of my younger years who I once gave myself to in the hope they perhaps would remain beside me on a day like this. I will remember hands, I always do, and wonder what they are doing now. Where have they planted themselves? Have they already passed through the great tunnel? Are they rooted in the palm of another or are they unlocked and free in some sensuous adventure? My breathing will grow weaker, lower, and the excitement from the school children outside will begin to wane. The song of my own dilapidating life will start its final call with each of my limbs preparing for their final dance. I will feel the hot iron of ruined love press down on my last exhalations and in that moment, irresolute and unpronounced, I will acquire the presentiment that one would rightly expect to supplement such fatalism. I will think of my son for one last time and my hands will shake, not with ailment or suffering but with an indomitable regret. I should have held him longer. Kept his hand in mine even when pride wouldn't permit it. I should have told him he was great and beautiful. Regret – the kind inspired by the lost chance of preserving just one of those giant loves from the fallen years, as I make my departure, bowing to the audience of life.

At the close of the last lament I will feel my chest heave, as if proving to the sky it's always been capable of supporting its own scale of universe. Tears will mar my sight, until those crowning seconds when a warm current of half-living blood will kiss each of my organs with one holy grace. A gentle goodbye. Done in the same way a dying flower may kneel upon the skin of the earth, showing its gratitude by whispering straight into the ears of its cosmic heart. Each section sharing an embrace, a final respect infused with an indebtedness fortified by the lone fact we were all permitted to die together. All the members of myself. Then, in that dreary room, with the din of wailing school-children having fully dissipated, and the world outside entering its vibrant restaurants and bistros, or releasing itself into the reaching arms of a lover, I will make my lone retreat.

Seventy-eight years ago I had a poor lonely woman greet me with her undying affection there in the arms she made for her first son. Lifting me out from inside her hot and clammy body, hampering my life with her naked flesh, whispering under joyous tears *you found me my beautiful darling.*

How was I to know, throughout those years, that everything would eventually culminate into something like this. Not even she, mother of all my life and blood, could have predicted the cruel and unbearable way the eyes and heart have to close forever.

Acknowledgements

The Blink That Killed The Eye wouldn't have been at all possible if it wasn't for the few hearts who played such an instrumental role in its creation. As often is the case with book acknowledgements one is unfortunately forced to whittle down the list of those who have either directly or indirectly influenced and spurred on the writing. In order to make that endeavour more exact and less laborious I thought to recall the names of those who've supported my writing throughout the various years, while simultaneously providing me with the courage and confidence to never let the ink dry up. To the distant reader these names may appear somewhat meaningless so I've attempted to add a sprinkling of detail to help show that behind everything there does exist someone who in some minuscule way helped with the writing of the stories in the book.

Many thanks to all the team at Jacaranda for wanting to publish the collection, it's been a tenuous road at times but we've made it to the end so for that I'm grateful. Thank you to the poet, the playwright and educator Joelle Taylor. For your insurmountable dedication to poetry and for being the first person to ever tell me I could write, deep within the Poetry Cafe basement some thirteen years ago. Thank you to my mother Hellen and my aunty Martha for constantly keeping the creativity and support alive throughout my childhood and through into my adulthood. Thank you to my father Tony for being my indefatigable financial pillar of support and most trusted counsel. Thank you to my brother Matthew and sister Stella for always being close by, even when at times the world seemed forlorn and distant. Thank you to my good friends at Out-Spoken; namely Daniel Randall a.k.a The Ruby Kid for joining me in our attempt to establish a congealed platform for both the performance of poetry and live music. To Karim Kamar for documenting the journey either through his camera, his monolithic keyboard or with his ingenious sense of humour, and also to Sam Bromfield for adding yet another strong hand to the never-ending labour of trying to keep art alive in the face of such apparent adversity. Thank you to Raymond Antrobus; a wonderful poet and dear friend who I deeply admire, one whose incessant fervour for poetry and education will forever amaze and inspire me. Thank you also to my agent Claudia Young at Greene & Heaton for making the whole experience as painless and as straightforward as possible given all the circumstances. Thank you to First Story who I've worked with for nearly three years. They are by far one of the greatest and most important initiatives in the UK today. An organisation who masterfully support and promote creative writing within schools around Britain, and a huge all-encompassing wave of appreciation for everyone who has in some shape or form inspired me over the years, be that through poetry, prose, song, theatre or conversation.

Lastly, I would like to say a very special thank you to Sabrina Mahfouz, the person who I wrote this collection for, indeed she was my singular audience. I doubt that in my lifetime I will encounter again an individual with such prodigious critical acumen. Not only is Sabrina an inimitable intellectual and philosopher but a fierce, unforgiving artist whose work challenges and comments on everything wrong within such a patriarchal heterosexual stratified society. I have learnt more from listening to her musings on gender inequality than I have from any academic study written by some far-removed theorising professor. Through the ten month writing period for *The Blink That Killed The Eye* she would scrupulously read over the stories, adding her notes and suggestions while listening to me ramble on about the book's philosophical intention coupled with my hopeless frustrations, my fears and pertinent anxieties. She was the reassuring voice when despair loomed and the motivational pick-up when fatigue brought me close to scrapping the whole damn thing. She was there from the inception of the title at a quaint port bar round the back of Oxford Circus, to the umpteenth reworking of the last sentence to the last story. Conclusively she is contained ubiquitously throughout these several narratives, and of course thank you to you dear reader, sincerely, for supporting these writings.